Carmen McRae

# "You're Afraid," He Said.

She nodded. "I've never done this before."

The back of his hand stroked her cheek. "Would you believe I haven't either?"

"No?" she asked, needing to hear his voice again.

"No." He paused to watch his fingers as they brushed across her brow, chasing wayward wisps of her auburn hair. "You're very lovely."

"So are you . . . handsome, that is."

"Does that mean you'll stay?" Urgency had suddenly overcome all else.

Reaching for her wrist, he drew her hand down to cover his heart while his other arm maintained its circle around her. She felt a strong beat, a thudding that might have been her own heart beneath her palm.

"Will you stay?" he asked again.

Would she reach for fantasy's fulfillment? Just this once? "Yes," Deanna heard herself murmur through lips that were moist and faintly trembling.

## BILLIE DOUGLASS

enjoys writing romances and confesses that her "family, friends and imagination" influence what ultimately comes from her typewriter. She spends hours at the library researching (backseat traveling) new and interesting locations. Ms. Douglass lives with her husband and three sons in Massachusetts.

Dear Reader:

SILHOUETTE DESIRE is an exciting new line of contemporary romances from Silhouette Books. During the past year, many Silhouette readers have written in telling us what other types of stories they'd like to read from Silhouette, and we've kept these comments and suggestions in mind in developing SILHOUETTE DESIRE.

DESIREs feature all of the elements you like to see in a romance, plus a more sensual, provocative story. So if you want to experience all the excitement, passion and joy of falling in love, then SILHOUETTE DESIRE is for you.

I hope you enjoy this book and all the wonderful stories to come from SILHOUETTE DESIRE. I'd appreciate any thoughts you'd like to share with us on new SILHOUETTE DESIRE, and I invite you to write to us at the address below:

Karen Solem
Editor-in-Chief
Silhouette Books
P.O. Box 769
New York, N.Y. 10019

# BILLIE DOUGLASS
## Beyond Fantasy

Silhouette Desire

Published by Silhouette Books New York

America's Publisher of Contemporary Romance

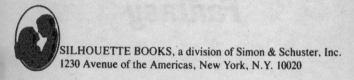

SILHOUETTE BOOKS, a division of Simon & Schuster, Inc.
1230 Avenue of the Americas, New York, N.Y. 10020

ISBN: 0-671-46826-X

First Silhouette Books printing July, 1983

10 9 8 7 6 5 4 3 2 1

America's Publisher of Contemporary Romance

Printed in the U.S.A.

**Other Silhouette Books by Billie Douglass**

# 1

"Good morning, Mrs. Hunt. Have you decided what you'll have for breakfast this morning?"

Deanna Hunt raised her eyes from the morning paper. With rare exceptions, she had eaten breakfast in the dining room of the Hunt International-Atlanta Hotel every morning for the past ten years. A menu was unnecessary.

"Any fresh strawberries today, Frank?" she asked softly.

Frank Pareto smiled and winked. "Fresh and sweet. With a little cream, perhaps?" he coaxed gently. In the years he'd been serving her, never once had he heard a condescending word pass her lips. Despite her youth, when Lawrence Hunt had married her and brought her to Atlanta to live, she had always been poised and gracious. Frank looked forward to her arrival in the dining room each morning. "The pecan rolls are particularly good today," he added on a note of temptation. "May I bring you a basket?"

Deanna returned his smile with a hint of chiding. "Are you trying to fatten me up, Frank?"

"That's my job, Mrs. Hunt." The waiter tipped his head, not in the least hesitant. As had many on the Hunt staff, he had grown more protective of her since the death of her husband nearly fourteen months earlier. She inspired that kind of caring.

"You do it very well." Deanna's compliment preceded a decisive nod. "Make it strawberries with cream and *one* pecan roll." She arched an auburn brow to emphasize the strict limit. Now that she had finally replaced the weight she'd lost after Larry's death, she no longer looked painfully thin. In fact, she had begun to notice gentle curves that had not been there when she'd first married. She had been nineteen then, barely out of her teens. Now she was several months short of thirty and a wealthy widow. It was a situation some women would have envied, yet Deanna increasingly sensed its flaws. With not a material worry in the world, she had no outward cause for complaint. What, then, explained the growing restlessness she felt?

Her disconcerted eye returned to the paper as Frank quietly disappeared into the kitchen and another waiter unobtrusively poured her coffee. He was a newer member of the hotel staff and slightly in awe of the presence of the head of the Hunt Foundation. Only Deanna knew her role to be a titular one. Like a queen, she was pampered and revered while the true power lay in the hands of others.

"Deanna?" A restrained male voice broke into her sober reverie, drawing her head up seconds before it brought a spontaneous smile to her lips.

"Jim, what a pleasure to see you!" she exclaimed,

warmly extending her hands to meet his clasp. "It's been a long time."

James Drummond was relieved by the welcome. Though he knew that Lawrence and Deanna had purposely formed the habit of breakfasting in the dining room in order to be accessible to the hotel's guests, he feared that he had caught Deanna in a moment of private thought. She had borne a look of utter vulnerability in that split second before the mask of the hostess had fallen over those deep inner emotions.

"I haven't been in Atlanta for months," Jim explained, releasing her slender hands slowly. "It seems that business has been concentrated around New York and Boston lately." He paused. "You're looking very well, Deanna."

"Thanks, Jim," she acknowledged his concern. "I'm doing well. The foundation goes on and I try to keep busy." Her eyes brightened. "How's Angie?"

At the mention of his wife, Jim smiled. Deanna had always been the perfect hostess, with a distinct knack for remembering such things as the name of the spouse of even a minor Hunt business associate such as himself. "Angie is just fine."

"And the boys? The youngest must be . . . getting ready for college?"

"Entering Duke University next month," he replied with renewed admiration for her memory. "He may just bring us in your direction more often."

Deanna's smile broadened. "I hope so. You'll make a point to stop back again soon, won't you?"

"Of course, Deanna," Jim assured her, sensing her sincerity. "Take care now." With a brief salute, he was gone. Deanna's smile dissipated with his departure and she looked absently around the dining room for other familiar faces.

Lawrence Hunt had believed in elegance and that was what he had created when he'd built the hotel fourteen years before. This formal dining room embodied an old-world charm that had been abandoned in much of modern Atlanta. Here one dined in low-keyed splendor beneath graceful crystal chandeliers while seated in high-backed armchairs and served on fine white linen, with exquisite china and silver. If the cost of such grandeur was nearly prohibitive, the guests were undaunted. They returned repeatedly to visit the Hunts.

Catching sight of a familiar face at a table across the room, she smiled and nodded, then dropped her gaze to frown at the crease that her pale pink fingernail had distractedly inscribed on the padded linen tablecloth. There were always people to see and things to be done. Her days didn't lack for activities of her choosing. So what could be lacking?

Frank arrived with her breakfast. As she moved her hand aside to make way for the ice-embedded bowl of strawberries, she chanced to glance toward the far corner of the dining room, where the sun streamed through graceful bay windows. In the echo of a heartbeat she stared. There was a new face, one she didn't recognize. Surely she would have remembered had she seen this man before, for he was quite striking as his eyes captured hers.

"Powdered sugar, Mrs. Hunt?" Frank interrupted, the sugar bowl in his hand, its spoon poised to sprinkle.

Deanna tore her gaze from that of the stranger. "No. No, thank you. Cream will be fine," she told him in the soft tone that now hid her uncertainty. Before she could reach for the small porcelain pitcher, Frank raised it and swirled its rich white contents over the ripe red berries. Cupping the empty vessel in his left hand, he used his right to nudge an opening between water goblet and coffee cup for the lone pecan roll she'd ordered and its small rose-shaped butter pat.

"Will there be anything else now?"

"This will be fine." She smiled her quiet appreciation and ever so subtle dismissal. She took her fork, then savored the sweet taste of several strawberries before venturing to look up again toward that far corner and that new face.

Eyes averted now, he read his own newspaper, his head bent. The morning sunlight filtered into the room, reflecting off the flatware before him and bouncing up to play among the chandeliers before spraying pale copper sparkles through hair that was every bit as thick and auburn as her own swept-up tresses, though far shorter. Even seated, he seemed tall and graced with dignity.

Deanna was held in his spell by the powerful masculine command he exuded. She helplessly admired his dark business suit, crisp yellow shirt and silk rep tie, all complementing his dark hair and bronzed skin perfectly. From a distance, she guessed him to be in his late thirties.

Despite her intent regard, the width of the room kept the fine details of his features hidden. Perhaps it was just as well, she realized with a jolt. For, while she would have liked to have examined him more closely, she found her interest new and frightening. He was different. Very different.

As his attention momentarily left the paper to focus on the plush burgundy carpet, Deanna felt an odd premonition. Then, as she had known he would, he lifted his gaze to meet hers directly and she felt strangely excited. The man was absolutely compelling. His expression contained an enigmatic blend of curiosity and vulnerability, all somehow rooted in a potential for strength that held her rapt for several long moments before she finally managed to force her eyes downward once more and slowly released the breath she'd been holding.

Her hand was less steady as she ate another strawberry, her thoughts on the riveting man with the most unusual expression on his face. He *was* different. But in what way? She had seen many attractive men come and go over the years, many just as charming, equally good-looking and as virile. What set this one apart from the others?

She sipped her coffee, not quite daring to confront him again. Looking in the opposite direction, she spotted a couple approaching and smiled quickly, grateful for the diversion. "LeeAnn and Tom! What a nice surprise!" Half rising, she offered a cheek to each of the pair in turn before sinking back into her chair.

LeeAnn Walker was an attractive brunette of roughly the same age as Deanna. The two women had been tennis partners for several years. "I couldn't resist showing you that he's actually taking me to breakfast," LeeAnn quipped, slipping her arm affectionately through her husband's as she looked at him. "We're doing it in style."

Deanna laughed. "I can't argue with that. How are you, Tom? I see your better half often enough, but not you," she scolded softly.

"That's because I'm busy earning the money to support not only the club membership but breakfasts at the choicest spots in town," Tom countered, not in the least disturbed by either expense. Deanna knew of the success of his law practice. The couple had recently moved into a new house, then shortly after had taken a trip to the Orient. She might have liked to have gone herself . . . had Larry been alive.

Determinedly thrusting aside the might-have-beens, she spoke to Tom. "LeeAnn tells me how well everything is going for you."

Tom's grin confirmed it. "Very well. And very busy. By

the way, I'm hoping to do some work with Jay Knowlton for your fund-raising drive." Jay Knowlton was chief legal counsel for the Hunt Foundation and the fund-raising drive in question was for a new children's hospital to be heavily endowed by the foundation.

"Really?" Deanna brightened. The hospital had become her pet project. "I didn't know that! Hmmph." She scowled in feigned exasperation, first at LeeAnn then back at Tom. "I'm often the last one to know these things." It had been happening more often than she'd like lately, and her exasperation was only half in jest. "I think that's great! We could really use your help—both of you!"

LeeAnn warded her off with a wave of her hand. "Don't look at me, Deanna. I've already enlisted."

"I know." Deanna smiled more gently. "And I'm pleased. It'll be fun working together." She meant it. Given her own quiet personality, good friends her age had been hard to find. While she was socially poised and knew the right things to say at the right times, she was, and had always been, a basically private person. The outwardly confident and polished woman she portrayed was a product of years of practice and loving encouragement, first on the part of her parents, then her husband. But her innate introversion had on occasion been mistaken for aloofness by her peers, keeping them at arm's length. LeeAnn and she, on the other hand, had formed a warm relationship and now spent the better part of three mornings a week together at the club playing tennis, enjoying a sauna and massage afterward. Both women accepted the fact that their social lives went in different directions, Larry's group had been older and now that he was gone, Deanna rarely went out.

The maître d' appeared by Tom's side. "Your table is ready, Mr. Walker."

13

LeeAnn grinned at Deanna. "I'll see you at ten?" It was Wednesday. Their standing court time was from ten to eleven.

"Sure thing, LeeAnn. It was great seeing you, Tom. Enjoy your breakfast."

LeeAnn swooped close with a stage whisper. "Any recommendations?"

Deanna shot a glance at her own plate. "I'm told that the pecan rolls are good today. I'm trying one. Why don't you order a basket?" she asked, grinning mischievously. "You can work it off later." It was a standing joke between the two. If Deanna was often two pounds short of ideal, LeeAnn was two beyond.

"Why don't *you* have the basket?" LeeAnn rejoined wryly, then followed the quip up with a gentle laugh that faded as she allowed herself to be led to her table. Tom's parting wave said they'd see her later. Once more, Deanna's smile slowly evaporated. She had never minded being alone. It was part of her personality. Why, then, did she now feel lonely?

On an inexplicable impulse, Deanna sought out that far corner of the room. A glimmer of anticipation passed through her, quickening her pulse. But the table was empty. The handsome stranger had left. Her hope faded as quickly as it had arisen. With a quiet sigh of resignation, she returned to her breakfast.

By the time she had finished her second leisurely cup of coffee, it was nearly nine o'clock. At her request, one to which he was accustomed, Frank bagged several additional pecan rolls, then held her chair as she stood to leave. For a brief minute he watched her go, silently admiring the class of this woman who was always so polite and soft-spoken. She might own the hotel, he mused, but there was not an ounce of arrogance in her.

Frank's wasn't the only eye to follow her departure. Almost everyone who knew her shared a similar admiration. She had survived Lawrence Hunt's sudden death with a dignity that would have made him proud and she now carried on the Hunt tradition he had worked so hard to establish.

She made a striking figure as she wove through the tables, smiling gently and nodding at one acquaintance or another on her way to the door. Slim and of an average height that was accentuated by strappy gray high-heeled sandals, she wore a cream-colored linen blouse with a loose V neck and generous billowing sleeves that were gathered at the wrist. Her skirt was of the peasant variety that no peasant could dream of affording, a rich mix of browns, grays and écrus that floated gracefully about her as she walked. The only jewelry she wore was a pair of simple gold earrings, a wide-banded gold necklace that lay flat on her bare throat and the plain gold wedding band she had taken a preference to wearing over the more elaborate rings her husband had bestowed on her. In her simplicity, she was as elegant as the dining room she left.

The hotel elevator quickly whipped her up to the fortieth floor, where she lived in the sumptuous suite that had been hers and Larry's through their nine plus years of married life. Friends had often wondered why they hadn't bought a spacious home in one of the suburbs of Atlanta. Larry had offered it to her more than once, but she knew he enjoyed the hotel. Perhaps if they'd had children they might have made the move. But children had never come and they'd remained here. It was as though Larry had known that then people would be around to look after her in his absence.

Deanna paused outside her door long enough to punch out the numerical combination to unlock it, then pushed it open and stepped into a wide foyer. "Irma?" she called once, then again more loudly as she closed the door and scanned the empty living room.

"Right here, Mrs. Hunt." Irma materialized instantly from the far end of the suite. She was a small bundle of energy in a gray and white starched uniform, the image of warm-blooded efficiency. "I was just changing the linens," she explained, stuffing the same into a pillow-case. Irma had served as Lawrence Hunt's housekeeper since he'd moved into the hotel. Her husband, Henry, was chauffeur, handyman and messenger wrapped into one wiry, white-haired package. They shared a smaller but still roomy suite conveniently adjoining the kitchen and their sole duty now was to see to Deanna's needs. On occasion, Deanna turned the tables.

"Here, Irma." She extended the bag of rolls toward the older woman. "Pecan rolls for you and Henry. They're delicious today." She leaned forward, listening. "Is he out already?" When Henry was at work cleaning or polishing around the suite, there was always a telltale sound to be heard, a whistling, a humming, even a scratchy chatter to himself. Now everything was quiet.

Irma tucked the pillowcase under her arm and accepted the bag. "He's gone ahead to the garage to polish the car. I'll give him a buzz when you're ready to leave. And . . . thank you for the rolls," she added with a self-conscious smile. "You really shouldn't bother yourself about us."

Deanna's cheeks dimpled as she squeezed the woman's arm gently. "Don't be silly, Irma. It was no bother. Enjoy them!"

"Oh, we will. Pecan rolls are Henry's favorites. But you knew that, didn't you?"

Deanna passed off the observation with a sheepish shrug, then began to move away. "I'll be working in the den for a little while. Will you have Henry bring the car around in half an hour?"

"Certainly. Your bag is all set to go. I'll bring it right out. Oh, and Mrs. Hunt?"

16

Halfway down the hall now, Deanna turned. "Uh-huh?"

"I thought I'd make a roast lamb for dinner. Is there anything special you'd like for lunch?"

Deanna considered the matter briefly before dismissing it and continuing down the hall. "Something light," she called back over her shoulder. "Perhaps an omelet?"

Irma smiled and shook her head at the disappearing figure. She knew just how Deanna Hunt liked her omelets: moist, with cheese and spinach. It was a simple meal to prepare. She half suspected that Deanna chose it often for that very reason. But Deanna was as undemanding in other things as well, which was remarkable, since she had grown up amid nearly as much wealth as she currently enjoyed.

Indeed, Irma mused, it would not have been surprising had she been spoiled and demanding, yet she was neither. She was an easy woman to please, her temper calm and controlled even during those times when her eyes held that well of loneliness she kept so stoically to herself. Through the months following her husband's death she had held her emotions in check. Now over a year had passed and she did no differently.

It seemed odd that a woman as young and attractive as Deanna Hunt should lead such a simple existence. Not quite the poor little rich girl, she was outwardly content. But surely she should be out more, with people, enjoying life. Surely she should be having fun, leading a less structured life than she did. Perhaps . . . in time. Shaking her head in silent regret, Irma headed for the laundry room.

Meanwhile, in the den, Deanna lifted her pen to write another of the letters she was personally sending to each of two hundred potentially major contributors to the hospital project. "Dear Monte and Diane," she wrote, then let the pen fall idle once more. Monte and Diane were friends of Larry's, contemporaries of his rather than hers. What were her own contemporaries doing with their lives?

More often now than ever in the past, she wondered what things might have been like had she gone on to college as her brother had, rather than marrying fresh out of high school and becoming Larry's wife and hostess. Certainly she would have formed a different, if smaller, circle of friends. She might even have married someone her own age rather than a man twenty years her senior whom her parents had known for years. Larry had courted her gently, offering her the care and protection she had come to depend on. He had loved her, and she him, but in a way that was somehow different from what she had imagined it to be in her wildest dreams.

In place of starbursts and rainbows she had found companionable serenity. While Larry lived, it had been enough. Now, as she faced a future alone, she wondered. What would it be like to do something wild? Something irresponsible? Something selfish? Could she ever kick up her heels and truly let loose? Her brother had done it and the results had been tragic.

Shaking her head free of the sad memories, Deanna grimaced at her inappropriate thoughts. She was simply not the rebellious type. Even had her brother not died so young, she probably would always have stayed close to home. After all, she did enjoy her life and its comforts. She couldn't deny that. And there was definite psychological merit in devoting oneself to philanthropic concerns such as those encompassed by the Hunt Foundation.

"Dear Monte and Diane . . ." She reread the salutation aloud, put pen to paper and proceeded to complete the letter from one of the prototypes she'd worked out with the public relations department. By the time she had finished and signed her name with a disciplined flourish, it was time to leave.

This Wednesday passed as did every other Wednesday. Henry dropped her at the club for the morning and picked her up later. She ate lunch back in her suite in the sunny, informal breakfast room, which was never used for breakfast, only for lunch and dinner. The larger, more formal dining room, which seated sixteen easily, had been unused for over a year.

Her afternoon was spent quietly at home, ostensibly heading the Hunt Foundation from the comfort of her den, in reality serving as a high-ranking social secretary. She received her customary call from Robert Warner, the executive director of the foundation, in whose hands true power rested. The call was filled with pleasant words regarding what she should be doing that day, what the next day's meeting would discuss and any small tidbits that Bob chose to pass on. There was, in fact, little substance to the conversation. But it had been that way for months. Why should Deanna be frustrated by it now?

She wrote ten more letters to add to the growing stack, kept up with other personal correspondence to one friend or another of Larry's who had dropped her a note, then made several phone calls on minor foundation business. She picked up the novel she'd bought the day before and read for an hour before dinner, then for several more after dinner, before bathing and retiring to begin again the next morning.

But this would be Thursday. Tuesdays and Thursdays held a special place in her heart. Though the afternoons were spent at the Hunt International offices several blocks away, the mornings were her own. Few people knew that she spent them in the pediatrics ward of the Atlanta General Hospital, talking with, reading to or sometimes simply holding those children whose parents could not be there. It filled a special need of hers and she would have given up almost any other activity before she gave up this one. There was an added lightness to her step when she entered the hotel dining room Thursday morning and took her regular table.

"Good morning, Mrs. Hunt." Frank welcomed her with a half bow and a smile. "How are you today?"

"Just fine, Frank." Deanna cocked her head in the direction from which she'd just come. "Was that a slice of honeydew I just passed?"

The waiter grinned. "It was."

"May I have one? And an order of cinnamon toast, please?"

"With honey?"

"Without honey." She cast him a humorous look that recalled the previous day's chiding and enough was said. Frank moved off, clearing the way for her to see to the far corner near the window. Instantly her senses came alive. *He* was there again, that tall, auburn-haired man, looking at her with that same profound expression that took her breath away. It hadn't occurred to her that he'd return— she hadn't allowed herself to think it. Yet there he was! Was he a guest at the hotel?

Fascinated by the unspoken depths of the stranger's gaze, Deanna couldn't look away. His presence tugged at her, evoking sensations of silent communication she'd never experienced before. His eyes said "Good morning" and hinted at a smile when hers returned the greeting. "Who are you?" he asked wordlessly, and "Where are you headed?"

"Here you are, Mrs. Hunt." A gleaming china plate bearing a generous wedge of succulent green melon was slid into place before her. Startled, Deanna snapped her attention back.

"Oh! Thank you, Frank," she murmured, then

breathed deeply to steady her pulse as she watched the waiter carefully set down a plate of toast with its heat-saving silver dome.

Who was that man? Deanna opened her mouth to ask Frank, but shut it just as quickly and let the waiter leave without another word. Only then did she scold herself for her foolishness. If Frank hadn't known the stranger's name he could easily have discovered it. Deanna often made similar requests when she couldn't find the name to fit a face she recognized.

But this was different. *He* was different. Hadn't she known it from the start? Though Deanna willed herself not to look up again, his face was indelibly etched in her mind. It was a strong yet gentle face, sun-touched and manly. Today his suit was of a lighter shade, a misty gray that emphasized the dark thickness of his hair and the even darker, deeper awareness in his eyes. Today the distance between them seemed to fade, bridged by an incredibly sensual familiarity. Absurd as she knew it to be, Deanna felt that she had known him for years. She stared at him, stunned by the force that flowed between them. It was as though they were emotionally tuned to one another. It was strange, but she sensed that he needed her.

Then she caught herself. That was ridiculous! She didn't know the man! Scoffing at her runaway imagination, she dragged her gaze downward and raised a spoon to the waiting melon. But she paused before making the first gouge that would mar the perfection of the slice. Was it ridiculous? Was there such a thing as an instant attraction that could explain the wild fluttering in her stomach? Wild fluttering? With a quiet chuckle of self-indulgence, she realized that this soft internal fluttering might be the wildest thing she would ever feel. And then she sucked in her breath as an even wilder thought titillated her senses. Blushing warmly, she forced it from her mind with a piercing thrust of her spoon into the melon's soft flesh.

Reaching for the morning paper which was always left for her, Deanna applied herself to the news of the day with greater intentness and less success than ever. Had Anthony Broad and his two out-of-town clients, the three old acquaintances of the Hunts, asked her what she'd read when they paused to greet her moments later, she might well have been embarrassed by her ignorance. But it didn't matter. Her purpose was served. She returned to the paper, ate breakfast with a painstakingly unhurried air, smiled at those who dropped by—all the while denying to herself the presence of that man and his startling effect on her.

As on the previous morning, the mystery man was gone long before Deanna finished. When she threw caution to the winds and glanced helplessly toward his table there was only a lingering sunbeam to mark where he had been. With a sigh that was as much of relief as disappointment, she forced herself to close the book on a short-lived fantasy. Decisively shouldering her bag, she headed directly for the spot in front of the hotel where Henry and the car were waiting.

The morning was as gratifying as she might have hoped, as rewarding as it was tiring. Henry picked her up at the hospital at noon and chauffeured her home for lunch, then delivered her an hour later to the executive offices of the Hunt Foundation, where she spent the afternoon in conference with various members of the foundation organization.

Bob Warner arranged these meetings as efficiently as he did most everything else. He offered Deanna only what information she needed to be generally aware of foundation activities, answered her questions patiently and gave his advice freely. He had been frankly startled when, soon after Larry's death, Deanna had asked to be given these regular briefings. With her total lack of business training, it might have been easier for her to have handed over the reins completely. But she had needed to participate in some small way, and though Bob's word was more often than not the law, her twice-weekly presence among the office staff carried a subtle and understated force. She was quiet and unobtrusive, but her questions were pithy, her inquiries pointed. She possessed good common sense and a knack for diplomacy, both of which Bob Warner channeled into useful avenues.

In this case the avenue was the drive toward the building of the Greater Georgia Children's Hospital and the bulk of the afternoon session revolved around the fund raising in which Deanna was already deeply involved. After much coaxing, she had finally agreed to hold a series of private dinner parties in her own suite, each courting eight to ten potentially significant supporters of the project. Though Bob and his wife would be at each, along with at least one or two other foundation bigwigs, Deanna had not entertained since Larry's death and never alone. As intimidating as the thought had been at first, Bob's argument was valid. There was an emotional value to be gained from Deanna's visible activity and Larry's vivid memory. It had been Larry's last hope to see this project a reality.

Deanna was exhausted when Henry finally shuttled her home at six. She ate alone, reflecting on the afternoon's meetings as Irma quietly served her a private feast of rock cornish hen and wild rice. Later she retreated to her bedroom to read before sinking at length into a restless sleep.

When she arose Friday morning it was with a vague sense of anticipation. She took greater pains in dressing than she had on either of the past two mornings. Even on tennis mornings such as this she would never have thought to show herself in the hotel dining room looking anything less than well groomed. Today, however, she wanted to do even better.

Sorting through the rack of late-summer fashions, she chose a pale lavender sundress, a one-piece wrap that was strapless, self-sashing and bottomed by gay white high-heeled sandals. Her jewelry was simple: small hoop earrings, a necklace, a ring. But she added an extra coat of mascara to her lashes, giving them the illusion of even greater length, and a second dab of color high on each cheekbone. As always, she swept her thick fall of dark copper-sheened hair loosely to the top of her head, securing it this time with an exquisite gold-leaf clasp before breaking from custom and pulling several tendrils free to wave delicately around her face and neck. With a touch of perfume to the pulse at her throat and the tossing of a lightweight open-weave blazer over her shoulders in deference to the potential chill of air conditioning, she was off.

Beneath the archway of the dining room, she took a deep breath to fill her lungs with confidence, then slowly let it out in the short walk to her table. She was met there by the maître d', whom she acknowledged with a smile. "Good morning, George."

"Good morning, Mrs. Hunt. Here, let me help you." He adjusted her chair as she sat down. "Enjoy your breakfast."

"Thank you," she said softly, casually reaching for the newspaper as he vanished. Her heart beat a rapid tattoo and she only prayed that she looked more normal than she felt. The news held no special appeal at the moment, but she focused on it to keep from looking elsewhere.

Frank approached quietly, his voice low. "Good morning, Mrs. Hunt. You look lovely today."

"Why, thank you, Frank." Would *he* think so too? The fantasy persisted! "It's kind of dreary out, though. Do you think it's going to rain?" With a perfect excuse she glanced toward the far window. He wasn't there! And it looked as though it would pour. Deanna felt suddenly gloomy herself.

Frank's gaze followed hers, though it encompassed only the elements beyond the large bay window. "They say we may get a few showers this morning. I hope you don't get caught in any."

Just then Deanna didn't care. She had looked forward to seeing that stranger again, and he wasn't there. Had he gone back to where he'd come from? Or simply gone elsewhere for breakfast? It had been fun dressing especially for him. But he'd let her down. Would she ever see him again?

Deanna's Friday proceeded as Mondays and Wednesdays did, with a morning at the club and an afternoon at home. But much as she threw herself into her prearranged activities, she couldn't shake the image of an auburn-haired man. In those few short moments of visual exchange, he had made her startlingly aware of something she had managed to ignore—that she was a woman, an individual, warm and alive.

It occurred to her as she analyzed it that she lived in a virtual cocoon, insulated and protected from the outside world. Every move she made, every person she met, was within the limited realm of this cocoon and she was invariably accorded the deference her position merited. To the world she was Mrs. Lawrence Hunt. Not so to this man.

It was one of the things that made him different. He had seen her as a human being, as a woman. His eyes had said as much. And he had shared a need she barely understood herself, had reached out to her with the force of his own inner drive. But he hadn't been back to see her today. Had their visual intimacy been no more than a figment of her imagination after all?

That imagination drove her to distraction. It was active all weekend through standing appointments at the beauty parlor and with the manicurist, a Saturday luncheon with a cousin who had stopped in Atlanta en route from St. Petersburg to Washington and Sunday afternoon's attendance at the wedding of the daughter of one of Larry's oldest friends. In between were moments of solitude, moments of intent contemplation, even brooding. She had sensed a growing void in her life, but this stranger's appearance had accentuated it. What was it she truly wanted?

Her thoughts became sensual daydreams, one as new and unexpected as the next and each involving the nameless vision of a tall, auburn-haired man. She pictured herself alone with him, lying beneath the shade of an ancient chestnut tree in a sylvan setting beyond the city. They talked of their lives and hopes, sharing fantasies without fear. Their only responsibility was to each other and she gloried in that singularity of purpose. Secluded in rural luxury, she held him, reveling in the hard strength beneath and against her that so desperately needed her softness for fulfillment. And he held her likewise, caressing her with a tender demand she still sought to comprehend. As the weekend passed, the dream soared higher and hotter until, aghast, Deanna forced the reality of solitude on herself once more. What *was* it she wanted? She refused to say.

Monday morning found her back to her routine and relieved to be busy once more. For the moment she was again content to fill the role in life she assumed had been meant for her. But when Tuesday morning came she was jolted out of her complacency when she glanced up from her French toast to find *him* looking at her. Her breathing faltered; her heart skipped a beat.

So he had returned! A ripple of excitement flowed through her veins and she felt suddenly freer, relieved of a burden she hadn't known she carried. He looked warm and wonderful, all tanned and handsome as he held her gaze unwaveringly. And then he smiled gently and she melted.

Deanna had never been as touched as she was by the silent reunion she shared with this man. She felt as though she'd found her special friend after a very long search, though the search had been solely in her fantasy life and had only spanned the four days since she'd seen him last. But he was flesh and blood, a far cry from imagination, and she knew that the vibrant awareness he sparked was no fantasy.

"Is everything all right, Mrs. Hunt?" Frank asked by her ear. Taken off guard, Deanna swung her head around abruptly and began to blush at having been caught in an uncharacteristic state of distraction.

"Uh, yes, everything's fine," she gasped quickly, then added on impulse, "but I wonder if you could do something for me?"

The waiter sobered in response to her gravity. "Of course."

Allowing herself no chance to back down, Deanna spoke directly. "There's a gentleman in the far corner. No, please don't look around now. He's sitting by the large bay window and has breakfasted here before. But I can't seem to recall his name or whether he's actually staying at the hotel. Could you possibly . . . ?" Her raised brows and softly pleading expression said the rest.

Frank's pleasure at the mission brought a conspiratorial smile to his lips. "Certainly, Mrs. Hunt. And I'll be discreet."

"You always are. I appreciate it." She paused awkwardly. "It's embarrassing . . . when I can't remember . . ."

"Please don't worry. I'll have the information you want in no time."

"No time" seemed to stretch on indefinitely as Deanna waited. She poked at her French toast, sipped her fresh-squeezed grapefruit juice, fingered the dull edge of the marmalade knife and tried to understand what it was this man stirred in her. It seemed to be a far-reaching passion that encompassed the emotional, the intellectual and, yes, the physical. The last was by far the most enigmatic. Why him? Why now? Or *was* she simply fantasizing that this stranger would be a panacea?

Daring to cast another glance his way, she found him staring solemnly out the window. What were his thoughts? she wondered as she hastened to freely admire the strength of his profile highlighted by the sun, the breadth of his shoulders beneath a fine-tailored navy blazer, the commanding air of his body even when seated and at ease. Who was he? she asked a final time and he must have heard, for he turned.

At that moment Deanna knew for certain that her need was not the only one. Despite her skepticism, she could not deny what she saw. His face held the same expression that had fascinated her that first day. It held a look of vulnerability, of searching, of loneliness. It seemed to beam a message that surged from his depths to penetrate his outer aura of composure. Deanna felt that he was asking *her* help—*she,* who had spent a lifetime on the receiving end of love, indulgence and protection. It frightened her, this gaze that pleaded with such dignity, yet she couldn't turn away from it.

Only the delivery to her plate of a small white card diverted her attention. She instantly knew that it was from the maître d's desk and reached to open it, her pulse hammering loudly, her teeth worrying her lower lip. For the same mystical reason that she was so drawn to the man, this information seemed crucial to her. She read the words as though her life depended on them.

Mark Birmingham. Architect with the firm of Birmingham and Swift, Inc., Savannah, Georgia. Registered at the Hunt International-Atlanta through Thursday.

Mark. First and foremost, Mark. A name for the face and a fitting one at that. Mark. Deanna spoke it silently several times, testing its strength in her mind and finding that it matched him well.

Mark. An architect. Obviously successful, most probably involved in a project requiring his midweek presence last week, now this. Smart man, she smiled in delight, to have chosen such a fine hotel!

Her smile was still in evidence when she looked up, but faded quickly at the sight of this smart man in the process of leaving. He stood taller than she had imagined and moved calmly and deliberately, with a liquid grace, toward the door. Her heart was in her throat as she helplessly watched him go. It was only at the last that he paused, head down, faltering. Then he looked up and made her day with a warm and gentle smile just for her before he disappeared into the hotel lobby.

Deanna let him go, somehow knowing she would see him again. For, whatever the long-range wisdom of it was, she knew that she *wanted* to see him again. If this was to be her first-in-a-lifetime stab at frivolity, so be it. Nothing could stop her from thinking of this man, from daydreaming and wondering what it might be like to be with him.

Cushioned by these daydreams, she passed the hours with a special spark to her smile. After a morning at the hospital she returned home for lunch, at the end of which she nonchalantly made the commitment she'd been toying with since breakfast.

"Irma, why don't you and Henry take the evening off? I think I'll eat downstairs tonight."

Irma's surprise was in direct proportion to the number of weeks it had been since Deanna had last done this. "Why, Mrs. Hunt, you don't have to do that on our account!"

"I know, but I'd like to eat in the dining room for a change. I've kept abreast of the breakfast crowd. Now it's about time I took a look at what goes on in the evening."

What Deanna had offered half in jest Irma interpreted quite differently. "It *would* be good for you to get out more. It's better that you be with people . . ." Fearing that she'd been too forward, she let her words trail off and scurried toward the kitchen. "If you should change your mind, just let me know," she called over her shoulder. "I can easily cook something up."

But Deanna had made her decision and notified the dining room of it on her way to the car. Though the late luncheon crowd was substantial, a cursory glance revealed no tall and auburn-headed architect among the lot. Perhaps he might be there tonight.

That, of course, was the motivating factor behind her deviation from habit and she was too honest to deny it. When Larry had been alive they'd taken the evening meal downstairs several times a week, in part to be accessible to friends and in part to be assured of the consistently fine quality of the restaurant. Since his death Deanna had preferred the nighttime sanctuary of her own suite on all but those few occasions when she accepted an invitation to be with a group. But an opportunity to see Mark Birmingham again was worth the effort of venturing forth and she was determined to do it.

Henry dropped her at the office at two and fetched her again at five. She spent the interim hours as usual, talking with different members of the foundation staff, then meeting alone with Bob to discuss and sign the inevitable stack of papers that required her formal approval. Bob was his usual patient self. If Deanna seemed to ask more questions than normal, to probe deeper into one decision or another than she had tended to do in the past, he accepted it all with good-natured indulgence. In turn, she graciously accepted his able explanations and the pat "Don't-worry-about-it's" and "It's-all-settled's" and "I'll-take-care-of-it's" he offered. He did have everything under control. For that, since her own mind was beginning to wander, she was grateful.

After returning home with Henry she settled into a bath filled to the brim with hot water and lemon-scented oil. An hour later she stood before the bathroom mirror with a towel wrapped sarong style around her. Before her was a woman she'd seen every day of her life. Or had she? Had she seen only part of the woman, that part that fit the image of the docile daughter and the loving wife? Was there another part she'd refused to see, a part that had only recently begun to beg for recognition?

Perplexed, she stared at her reflection. Her face was devoid of all makeup, yet it was bright and tingling with a hint of pink from the heat of the bath. Her hair was piled high, but loose wisps rebelled against restraint and curled gently toward her shoulders where the skin was moist, creamy smooth and soft. In a moment of curiosity Deanna reached for the point above her breast where the towel was tucked, pulled its end loose and slowly let it fall. Then, almost timidly, she looked at her body in a wholly new light. It was the body of a woman, with firm, full breasts and a narrow waist, a flat stomach and gently curving hips. Her legs were long and slim and of the same satin texture as the rest of her.

Slowly and with a dawning awareness, Deanna let her eyes retrace the route, moving intently upward. Would *he* admire her body as she had just done? Would he want to see it? To touch it? To know it? Her fingers were unsure as she lifted them to her breast, where they lay against the wild beat of her heart. Would *he* desire her as she'd long ago dreamed to be desired?

Larry had loved her as a husband loved a wife, but without any of the passion she'd once dared to imagine. And she had neither questioned his lack of demand nor her own passive acceptance of it, because she had been young, innocent and naive, contenting herself with his evident satisfaction, finding pleasure in the overall tranquillity of their lives and the orderly show of love that compensated for unleashed passion.

Unleashed passion. Was that what she craved? Would she know what to do with it? How to handle it? Sighing, she stooped to lift the towel from the floor and wrap it around herself as she passed through to her room in search of underclothes. Unleashed passion, hah! The only thing to be unleashed this day was a very naughty fancy that was destined for frustration. With a swift if rueful headshake she cast the thought aside.

But eight o'clock found her dressed nonetheless and on her way to the hotel dining room as she had preordained. She wore a dress of black silk that was soft yet sophisticated, scooped at the neck and draping her body with just enough fullness to suggest the fragile femininity within. There were solitary pearls at her ears, a fine strand around her throat and an exquisite wristlet to match the delicate gold-and-pearl creation she wore on the third finger of her left hand. Her hair was caught up with twin clasps of silk, her makeup blended with a light but skillful hand. In an utterly unaffected way she carried with her an aura of distinction as she smiled at the maître d' and preceded him to her table.

Far beneath this stunning surface she quivered, however, filled with trepidation that *he* wouldn't be there. It was a grand shot in the dark that she had made and she suddenly wondered why she had ever allowed her fantasy such freedom. Some dreams were meant to remain no more than dreams. Perhaps this was one of them.

"Enjoy your dinner, Mrs. Hunt." The maître d's parting words inspired her. Mark Birmingham or no, she was going to try. Settling into her chair, she took several deep and calming breaths. But she was unable to appreciate the grace around her, the soft notes of the piano as its music strove to soothe her mind, the flicker of a slender candle bringing to life the brandy-hued rose that stood proudly before her in its sterling bud vase. Opening her menu, she made a pretense of studying the elaborate list of offerings. But the exotic titles merged meaninglessly into one another; her mind was very definitely elsewhere. Finally, unable to restrain herself, she risked a glance up through the shade of her lashes toward his corner, where evening's atmospheric lighting had replaced the morning's sun.

Deanna raised her head higher and opened her eyes with the breathless realization that Mark Birmingham was at his table, nursing a drink and infinitely aware of her own arrival. His dark eyes locked with hers and he smiled a greeting. She smiled back almost shyly, lingering for a moment's pleasure before lowering her gaze in defense against the potent attraction she felt. But her brown eyes sparkled, her cheeks glowed, the pulse at her neck throbbed in excitement. It was an auspicious start for dinner, indeed, for the night itself.

Deanna barely knew what she ordered or ate, only that it was the most delicious meal she'd had in months. The service itself was faultless, its pace properly relaxed to allow her to greet friends and the occasional well-wisher, as well as indulge in periodic visual exchanges with Mark. At some point she actually wondered why they kept their distance, why one didn't approach the other and end their separation. But then her mind moved one step further and she was suddenly frightened. Fantasy was one thing, reality another. What if her dream man turned out to be a bore? Worse, a brute? What if his teeth were false or his hair sewn on or the breadth of his shoulders artificial? What if, when she finally heard it, his voice had a high nasal twang? As it stood, he had at least the illusion of perfection. Did she dare jeopardize the vision? No, some dreams were better left untouched. But the thought of *that* saddened her even more. She *did* want to touch Mark Birmingham . . . and that was the least of it!

It seemed it wasn't to be. Deanna had barely begun to sip her coffee when Mark rose from his table, sent her a last soulful stare and, to her disappointment, left the dining room. Her pleasure in her evening suddenly faded. Within minutes she followed his example, graciously thanking and complimenting the dining-room staff, then walking to the elevator, head down in thought.

She wasn't quite sure of the moment when he approached because there were other people quietly milling about. But something drew her head up and she found herself face-to-face with him. Her breath caught in a quiet gasp. At close range he was that much taller, that much more handsome, that much more intense. And his effect on her was staggering, the reality of him something to behold.

For the first time his features were near enough to study and know. His nose was strong, with a faint crook at its bridge, his lips firm and masculine, his jaw square and clean-shaven. The eyes she had only known to be dark now revealed themselves as a deep charcoal brown, and they were studying her just as intently as she was studying him. His hair was thick and rich and entirely his own, his chest broad enough to fill his jacket on its own sinewed merit. And when his lips curved in the hint of a smile she saw that his teeth had just enough of an irregularity to vouch for their authenticity. He was every bit the real thing. And she couldn't restrain a sigh.

At that moment the elevator arrived, demanding their immediate attention. But when Deanna felt a hand lightly take her elbow she knew it was Mark's. He held her back to let several others enter, then gently guided her aboard. Though his hand fell away she stayed by his side as the car whirred upward.

At the tenth floor one couple disembarked, at the eighteenth floor another. By the time the elevator left the twenty-seventh floor Deanna and Mark were alone. She stared expectantly at the lighted panel above the doors, watching the floors pass. Thirty. Thirty-one. Had she even pressed her own? Thirty-three. Thirty-four. Thirty-five. The car hummed to a halt and its doors slid back. As she held her breath she felt her hand taken by a larger, warmer, surer one. Taking courage from it, she met Mark's gaze. It held every bit of her own need and want, plus a sense of promise she hadn't seen before. His eyes silently offered the same invitation conveyed by his hand as, still holding hers, he stepped tentatively forward. Deanna hesitated for a final moment. Then, seized by an overpowering urgency, she followed him.

# 2

~~~~~~~~~~~~~~~~~~~~~~~

**W**hen the door to his suite quietly and irrevocably shut out the rest of the world, Mark drew her around to face him. He stood no more than a gasp away, tall and dark and silently demanding. In a fleeting moment of panic Deanna wondered where she was, why she was there, whether she could even begin to give this man what she knew he wanted. He was so real now. For the first time in her life she felt totally inadequate.

Reading the fear in her large fawn eyes, Mark moved to ease it. He raised his hands to touch her face, framing it with long, adoring fingers that wove lightly into her hair and tipped her features back for his tender exploration. His melting gaze transmitted wordless reassurance that she was everything he wanted and more. Gaining courage, Deanna held her breath in anticipation of the moment.

Release came with the slow lowering of his head and the soft touch of his lips against hers. She closed her eyes, timidly yielding to a new realm of sensation that bridged the gap between fantasy and reality. His mouth moved so lightly at first that she wondered on which side of that chasm she remained. But as the pressure increased slowly, demanding her response, Deanna knew that this kiss was no dream. There was nothing paternal or protective about it, nothing token or simply affectionate. As it deepened, it became a thing of passion, a kiss such as she'd never experienced before. And it induced the rising surge of an echoing need that in turn triggered her response.

But that response was tempered by the newness of it all; Deanna had never been so stirred before. Beneath Mark's sensual caress she relaxed her lips at first, moving them experimentally against their firm male counterparts, then gradually lost herself in the pleasure until she was as caught up in the mindless play as he was. It was indeed fantasy, and she yielded to its glory. She knew nothing but the euphoria of this man's touch.

With a ragged catch in his breath, Mark gently drew back his head. It was only when his hands fell to encircle her waist that Deanna realized that her own were clinging to his shoulders. She slid them to his back as he drew her tight against him. It was the first time their bodies had touched.

"Hi," he whispered, his smile bright.

Deanna gathered the bare remnants of breath he'd left her to falteringly whisper back, "Hi, yourself."

"Do you know," he pressed her closer, "that that's been a fantasy of mine?" It was still a whisper. She had yet to really hear his voice.

"What has?"

"To say hello for the very first time with a kiss." Where his manner might have held triumph or arrogance, there was only pleasure.

Deanna's face was a rosy reflection of that pleasure

even as she softly corrected him. "But you have said hello before . . ." she began, remembering those first visual greetings before fearing once again that she might have imagined them. But she hadn't.

Mark's eyes twinkled. "You heard me?"

"I heard you."

He softly sighed his relief. "I'm glad."

Unable to think of anything to say, Deanna simply nodded her agreement. The situation was mind-boggling. Though she stood in the arms of a stranger, she felt as close to him as she had to . . . to Larry. But Larry was gone and this closeness was different. She needed it every bit as badly as she'd ever needed anything. It was fantasy, yet it was tangible.

Mark's face took on the same look of vulnerability, the same intense need Deanna had fallen prey to on that very first morning nearly a week earlier. Looking up at his sun-grazed features, she was tossed about on an ocean of sensation. His body warmth buoyed her. The distinctive scent of man and brandy excited her beyond reason.

When his eyes finally captured hers they held the question she had already heard from his body, which tautened against her as he exercised control. Deanna fought an instinctive resurgence of fear. Mark wanted her. As a woman. Now. It was fantasy of the highest order. But it was an unknown. Had she thought it would go so far? How could it *not!* Her body trembled in anticipation.

"You're afraid," he stated in a deep and warmly understanding tone.

She nodded. "I've never done this before."

The back of his hand stroked her cheek, the contrast in texture somehow symbolic of their vibrant differences. "Would you believe that I haven't either?"

The issue wasn't virginity and they both knew it. Their silent understanding was that it was the suddenness of it all, as well as its force, that was unique. Calmed by his touch and gratified by his words, Deanna finally assimilated the rich timbre of his voice. It vibrated softly through her.

"No?" she asked, needing to hear it again.

"No." He paused to allow his fingers to brush across her brow, chasing wayward wisps of her auburn hair. "You're very lovely."

It was a standard line that Deanna had heard over and over again. But Mark had said it differently, with an intimacy that nurtured her delight. The words were offered freely and without obligation. And it was in precisely that spirit that she responded, with a slight blush and a hint of shyness.

"So are you . . . handsome, that is."

"Does that mean you'll stay?" Urgency had suddenly overcome all else.

"Does one necessarily go with the other?"

"If it's the only reason you can find."

"It's not." The exchange had been made in eager whispers. Now she felt her pulse accelerate more dangerously and wondered whether Mark could feel it. Could she ever be a sophisticated lover for him?

He reached for her wrist, then drew her hand down to cover his heart while his other arm maintained its circle around her. She felt a strong beat, a thudding that matched her own heart's rhythm, and its strength surged through her.

"Will you stay?" he asked again.

Would she reach for fantasy's fulfillment? Just this once? "Yes," Deanna heard herself murmur through lips that were moist and faintly trembling. She knew that she might live to regret what she was about to do, that in guilt alone she might suffer long after. She also knew that she owed this to herself. The feelings Mark inspired were too beautiful to be ignored. For the first time in her life she would be her own woman, responsible to no one but herself. And to *him*. Yes, that was the other half of her need. It was a need to give of herself to another. Here there was no question of the impersonal acts of letter writing or check signing or handshaking. She was no longer an adjunct of some larger body. Here she was a woman stripped of all pretense. Here she would have only that which was deep within her to give. It was a dazzling, if fearful, thought.

Again Mark felt her emotions. "We'll be together," he whispered and Deanna knew what he meant. He would help her, guide her. He didn't want her to be afraid.

With a smile, she nodded. His body felt fine against hers and she knew it would support her if she wavered. When he lowered his head to kiss her again she met him with lips parted in readiness. Passivity would not do for this man any more than it would do for the woman he seemed determined to make her. More than anything, she wanted to be that woman.

Standing back, he took her hand, then led her silently into the adjoining bedroom. Leaving her just past the threshold, he moved to turn on the lamp by the bed. Despite the many times she'd seen these rooms or others just like them, Deanna suddenly took them in in an entirely new light. The queen-size bed with its elaborate mahogany frame, the original silk-screen prints on the walls, the textured silk draperies and spread that shimmered shades of apricot and teal through the air—all were now a romantic backdrop whose details blended in sensual array.

The only details that stood out boldly were those of Mark's frame as he slowly turned to face her. Deanna was aware of the distance separating them and couldn't seem to make her feet move. Unsure as to what she should do, she watched silently as he shrugged out of his blazer and let it fall to the nearby armchair, then loosened his tie. His eyes held hers reassuringly, telling her that he would call when it was time. Deanna wondered at the steadiness of his hand as it released the top two buttons of his shirt, for she was anything but steady as the tanned V of flesh appeared. It was a narrow stretch, but enticing. She wanted to touch it, but held herself back, because the urge itself intimidated her. Once again his expression was of understanding and reassurance. But he made no move to stop.

She watched wide-eyed as each successive button was undone until he tugged at his shirttails and freed them completely from his pants, but kept the shirt on. In a moment of nervous anticipation Deanna moistened her lips. Her pulse raced and her limbs felt weak, but she could no more look away than she could turn her back on this man. With the soft closing of the door to his suite a few minutes before, she had been committed. That was what she wanted to be, wasn't it? One look at the wider expanse of flesh now exposed and she identified a part of those yearnings she had previously ignored. She wanted him physically as much as he wanted her. With the real world, that other world, now safely blotted out, she could freely admit that need.

Deanna sought the doorjamb behind her for support as her gaze slowly fell from his throat past a path of tanned, man-haired skin to the point at his waist where his hands now moved. After releasing his belt buckle, he unfastened his slacks and let them drop. Before she could catch her breath, he stood before her wearing nothing but the open yellow shirt with its tie draped loose and a pair of the bluest, sexiest continental-styled briefs she had ever seen.

In the instant's shock she felt totally out of touch. Was this the kind of underwear that men now wore? Men's underwear had never been an issue to consider in the past. Even as she helplessly stared at his body she tried to recall how inconsequential a matter it was. But it wasn't! Those snug blue briefs made a bold statement.

Deanna had never imagined that a man could be so physically exciting. Even her fantasy paled in comparison. As her gaze wandered her breath came faster. She traced his legs, long lengths of bronze, softly haired. She appreciated the perfect shaping of his calves and the latent power of his thighs. In the dim amber lighting he seemed ever warmer and more beckoning.

She gasped at the inevitability of what was about to happen. He called silently and she slowly left the doorway.

To say that she was in a trance would have been wrong, for she knew precisely what she was doing. She was living out a fantasy. She covered new ground with each step across the plush blue carpet. Never before had she been driven by the fire that now consumed all sane thought. Mark was the only one capable of quenching the flame and she walked steadily forward.

Inches away from him, she paused. Was this right? Was it what he wanted? He nodded almost imperceptibly and she raised her hand to touch his chest. His skin was warm to the touch and softly textured beneath her fingers. She nearly gasped at the delight of him, but bit her lip cautiously. Despite what he'd said about never having lived this particular dream before, Deanna knew that he had to be far more experienced in the ways of women than she was in the ways of men. While the sensations she felt were new to her, he had to know just what he wanted and how he wanted it done. There was nothing clinical about it; it was a simple matter of personal desire. Could she satisfy him?

"That's right," he murmured in encouragement when she moved her hand against his chest. Emboldened and curious, she brought the other to meet it, then began a tactile exploration that built her own arousal. With each passing second her fingers grew more eager, raking slowly across his chest to outline its muscled expanse. Again she looked up at him and again he spoke softly. "That's it. Feel free . . ."

He sucked in his breath when her fingertips breezed across each flat male nipple, then returned for a more brazen caress that produced dual bold buds. Deanna felt a definite sense of triumph at his instant response, yet her hands trembled all the more.

His hands gently encircling her neck, Mark tipped her chin up with his thumbs. "Don't be afraid to touch me," he whispered. "Anything is all right as long as you feel the pleasure."

Deanna slid her hands beneath the flaps of his open shirt and savored the smooth flesh of his sides from rib to hip. "And your pleasure . . . ?"

"Comes from you." He smiled with a gentleness that belied the smoldering light in his eyes. "Don't you see? Your pleasure brings me mine. They're one and the same. I don't think we could separate them if we tried."

"But I don't know . . ." she cried out softly in an attempt to confess her inexperience.

Mark wouldn't hear of it. "You *do* know." He was deeply insistent. "I saw it in your eyes from the first. You're exquisite." To illustrate his point he kissed her again, with greater conviction now and an ever-deepening drive.

Deanna found herself settling happily into the haven of his arms, surrendering willingly to the beauty of his kiss. This was part of that promise she had seen in *his* eyes and its soul-touch was every bit as exquisite as he claimed her to be. She submitted to his sweeping exploration of her mouth and thrilled to the heady nectar of his.

But again, from deep within the fantasy, came a

demand for more than submission. It wasn't enough to be kissed. Kissing back was just as critical. Under the gentle caress of his hands on the rustling silk that covered her back, Deanna opened her lips more fully to welcome Mark's tongue and then, timidly at first, meet it with her own. Gradually she experienced the sensation and soon found herself swept up in it. It was a whirlpool of desire, ever widening to draw her deeper and deeper into its heart. With growing abandon she let herself know its dizzying force as she met Mark's heat with her own.

He was right, she realized. The more she gave, the more impassioned she grew. It was an endless circle, as endless as the rings whirling about them, tightening bit by bit to bind them together.

For a fleeting moment Deanna wondered whether other women knew this extreme sensual joy, whether she was the oddity for having been ignorant of its bliss for so many, many years. She had always found satisfaction in other realms. Now, at this moment, there was only Mark.

As though hearing his name in her thoughts, he drew back to look at her. The familiarity of his expression was nearly more than she could bear. It spoke so clearly of his desperate need of her. But Deanna had just begun to recognize her own needs. This freedom he had given her was just taking root.

Moving on pure instinct, she leaned lower and put her lips against his chest. His skin seemed to throb beneath her mouth and she closed her eyes to better savor his scent and the wild heat he exuded.

He moaned, pressing her closer. She was aware of the full length of him, of the thighs that supported hers and the hands that molded her lower body to his. Her heart hammered loudly as she understood the rising thrust of his need. It, in turn, inflamed her.

Once again he held her back, this time with a hand on

her either arm. "I need you," he whispered. "It seems as if I've waited forever."

"I know," she answered falteringly, and she did. Fantasy had its own needs and they were demanding after their long years of denial. Breathing in short, uneven gasps, she gently nudged his shirt over his shoulders and let it drop behind him. But when she reached to touch the masculine wealth suddenly opened to her, he reached as well. She was unprepared for the sudden rush of air on her back, needing a minute to realize that he'd lowered the zipper of her dress.

Startled, she recoiled. There had been an unreality to the situation when he had undressed before her and her mind had been caught up in the passion of it all. But now it was her turn. Her clothing was the property of Mrs. Lawrence Hunt. Stripped of it, she was in many ways a stranger to herself.

"Please, let me love you," Mark said softly. "I won't hurt you. You know that, don't you?"

She nodded slowly. She did know it, though she wasn't sure how. When it came down to facts, she knew practically nothing about this man other than his name, his profession, his home base. He could be any number of horrible things . . . but she somehow knew he wasn't. As bizarre as it was, she trusted him. And she wanted him. Even in the throes of unsureness, she was aware of the fever that raged within her own body. There was only one antidote.

Forcing herself to relax, she smiled. "I'm all right. This is just so . . . new . . ."

"I know," he murmured, leaning forward to kiss her with the gentleness of that understanding. As he straightened he drew the dress from her shoulders and eased it down her body.

Deanna focused on the auburn vibrancy of his hair

while he knelt to help her from her black silk slip, her shoes, her stockings. With each went a bit of the past, replaced by the fantasy of a new woman. If the mild unsteadiness of Mark's hands was a sign of his own dubious control, Deanna's pulse was racing too fast for her to notice. Finally he straightened and looked down at her.

His eyes touched her everywhere, caressing her throat and the swells of her breasts, moving over her stomach to the lace-edged silk of her panties. She felt the heat rise to paint her cheeks a delicate pink as she tried to discern his thoughts. Was he disappointed?

Groaning softly, he gathered her into his arms. "How did I ever find you?" he rasped into her hair and she felt the beginnings of a reassurance that was enhanced by his hoarse-whispered, "So lovely." Working his way around her ear, he tasted the lemon freshness of her neck, then sought her throat in a sequence of warm, moist kisses. Deanna closed her eyes and let her head fall back as she felt resurging delight at every touch point. She arched her back unknowingly, innocently offering herself to him. The whisper of a sigh escaped her lips when his moved across her chest. Behind her, the muscles of his arms tensed with wanting.

In one dizzying moment she was lifted and gently laid on the bed. When she opened her eyes in the stillness, he was smiling just above her.

"Are you okay?" he asked. The arms he propped on either side of her trembled slightly.

"I think so." Reaching up, she threaded her slender fingers into the thickness of his hair and drew his face down. When she arched off the sheets to kiss him, he slid his hands behind her and deftly released the catch of her bra. It was gone in an instant and she gasped.

But the gasp caught in her throat, silenced by the worshipfulness of his expression. In its wake she felt like a goddess, a woman of flesh and curves with the awesome power to please this man. It was what she wanted more than anything to do. And she sensed a renewed urgency in him.

Her hands went to his shoulders, then around his neck, as she pulled herself into his embrace. His back was warm with muscles that flexed when she touched them, which she did with growing courage. But Mark touched as well, and was soon dissatisfied with the slender span of her ivory-sheened back. Easing her down he placed both hands on her neck, then began an erotic descent toward her breasts. When he reached their fullness at last, she strained toward him. Her nipples had long since grown taut, yet now they responded even more fully to him. His fingers massaged the pebbled tips until she bit her lip to keep from crying out at the torment.

"Don't do that," he commanded softly against her lips as his freed them from her teeth. "Yell, scream if you want to. I don't want you to hold anything back."

Deanna looked up. "I've never felt anything like this."

"I know." He grinned with a pleasure that was remarkably calm in light of the fire that licked at them both.

In that instant time sped back. Deanna recalled that fantasy of girlhood innocence when she'd first anticipated a man's possession. Blushing as she might have done then, she asked, "You do?"

"Uh-huh," he hummed smoothly, invitingly.

"How?" Without realizing it, she flexed her fingers around the solid strength of his arms.

"Your reaction. It's almost . . . virginal."

Embarrassed, she looked away. But Mark captured her chin and turned it back. He was sober and intense, silently speaking of that ultimate need. With a soft cry, the first she had allowed, she threw herself into his arms and moved restlessly against him.

It was as though she had given the sign; suddenly his

47

seduction began in earnest. He touched her everywhere, finding sensitive niches all over her body, kissing some, tonguing others, stroking them until she writhed beneath him. He paused only long enough to remove her panties, then his own briefs, before settling sensuously against her and letting her know the height of his desire.

Patience was exhausted on both of their parts. For Mark, the physical demand had overcome all other thought. For Deanna, all other thought was actively chased away. Her total concentration was on her body and his, on his hands that caressed her and hers that mirrored the motion. With each sound she made he gave her encouragement, and she felt freer than she had ever felt before.

There ceased to exist any other world, any other woman. The Deanna Hunt who lay on the bed, naked beside him, bore no resemblance to the Deanna Hunt who had existed for the past twenty-nine years. This Deanna was beyond all recollection of that other, more subdued woman. This Deanna was alive with love.

In a moment of passion that she would always remember, Mark moved above her, hesitated for a bare moment, then joined their bodies with a fluid grace that shimmered from one to the other and back.

"Ahhhh . . ." Deanna cried, unaware of the vocal sigh until it was repeated when he began to move in gentle rhythm. She clung to him as he held her closer and arched her hips to meet his thrusts, answering his need with the force of her intuitive femininity.

Later she would recall the soft words he said, the growing breathlessness, the coaxing sounds and cries. Now she was embroiled in the pleasure as it built slowly toward an apex she had never, ever known.

Mark was the consummate lover, never quite lost enough in his own passion to totally forget her greater vulnerability. With infinite care he led her upward, teasing and withholding, speeding and slowing until he felt her at the peak of her endurance. Only then did he offer her the release she blindly sought. At that mind-shattering instant she exploded with the fire of a thousand brilliant starbursts of the kind she had so secretly dreamed of long ago. Mark heard her triumphant cry and let it trigger his own as he gave in at last to that same supreme pleasure. It was a shared moment, a moment of ecstasy. Gasping raggedly, he crushed her against him until the last of the spasms subsided.

Deanna was enraptured. Her body seemed to float, held to earth only by the arms she coiled tightly around Mark's neck. She hadn't imagined that anything could be so perfect, so natural, so naked in its glory. For those few fleeting moments she had captured the fantasy of loving and being loved back to mindless distraction. She had discovered a primal luxury and its vivid force stunned her.

Needing to feel the reality of this man who had pleasured her so exquisitely, she stroked the dampness of his back until her fingers dropped to splay over the meeting of their hips.

"Deanna . . . Deanna . . ." Unknowingly Mark cried her name. His tone was hushed, his head buried against her neck as the beauty of passion lingered. But reason returned with a jolt when he realized that she lay suddenly still beneath him, her body incongruously tense.

# 3

**D**eanna?" Mark raised his dark head to look at her with concern. "What is it?"

The fury of passion had left her looking windblown. Having escaped its bounds, her thick auburn hair lay in billowing sprays, dark against the white of the pillow. Her skin was damp. Even the glow of lovemaking couldn't hide its sudden pallor. She stared at him fixedly, blinking only when he repeated his demand more urgently.

"Tell me, honey. What's wrong?"

It seemed forever before she was able to speak. Even her shock had not overcome that lingering breathlessness. "You know who I am," she said faintly. He had called her by name.

"Of course I know who you are."

"I didn't . . . expect that."

"Why not? You know who I am, don't you?" he chided her softly.

Deanna sank her teeth into her lower lip. Had she actually cried out his name too, without knowing it? She tried to think back to those last cataclysmic moments, but could hardly assimilate the overall magnificence of the fire that had consumed her so totally.

Mark nodded silently in answer to her inner question. "You spoke my name as unconsciously as I just spoke yours." He smiled. "It was very natural." Bending his head, he kissed tiny beads of moisture from her nose, then carefully slid to her side. Deanna seized the opportunity to turn her back and try to rise, but Mark caught her. His arm curved around her waist and gently drew her back, flattening her on the bed beside him.

"Oh, no, you don't! Now that I've found you, you can't up and leave me just like that."

Deanna avoided his gaze. "I've got to go."

"Do you?" he asked, arching a brow in doubt. "Is there someone expecting you? Someone waiting for you at this hour?"

Her eyes sent a message of mild rebuke as she looked toward him. "You should know the answer to that."

Undaunted, he reached to smooth a lock of damp hair from her cheek. "I know that you're Deanna Hunt."

She eyed him fearfully. Would he destroy the entire fantasy? "What else do you know about me?"

He grinned. "You live upstairs," he offered. As his smile continued to toy with his lips, Deanna felt herself melting all over again. In self-defense she focused on his chest, only to find it as unnerving as his smile had been.

His fingers fell from her cheek to curve lightly around her shoulder in a caress that was enough to remind Deanna of her nudity. Looking down, she groped for the sheet, but Mark caught her hand and stilled her. "Don't . . ." he gasped quickly, without thinking, then forced himself to relax. "Wait . . . it's all right."

She was suddenly overwhelmed by where she was and what she'd done. "It's not!" she cried. "This shouldn't have happened. I've got to leave."

"We've got to talk," he contradicted her.

"I can't." Pulling roughly away, she reached the far side of the bed, but a strange languor prevented her from standing up. As her confusion grew she wrapped her arms around her middle and swayed slightly back and forth. Before she could react to the dip of the mattress immediately behind her, a second pair of arms appeared to cover hers and she was drawn back into a virile cradle.

"I won't let you go until we've talked." Deanna hung her head and slowly shook it in dismay. "Please talk to me," he repeated, near pleading.

But her thoughts remained her own. *What had she done?* How had she come to find herself here? How could she have allowed herself this lapse of judgment? After all, she was Mrs.—

"Then you'll *listen* to me." Mark cut firmly into her self-reproach, holding her unyieldingly yet softly enough to give whatever comfort he could impart. "I know that you're Deanna Hunt and that you live here at the hotel. My waiter was kind enough to tell me that. The rest I figured out for myself."

"The rest?" she asked hesitantly.

He sighed and tightened his arms a fraction. "You're Lawrence Hunt's widow." She drew in her breath and tried to escape, but he refused to release her. "This hotel is yours, as is that shiny limousine outside, not to mention the corporation your husband founded."

The voice that had been so close by her ear grew silent until Deanna could hear nothing but the guilty thud of her heart. When he spoke again she caught a touch of humor. "Did you really hope to remain anonymous?" He paused, then gently squeezed her. "Hmmm?"

"I don't know," she whispered at last.

With a pained moan Mark shifted her until she sat sideways in his embrace. "Would you like to know what else I've learned about you?" he asked in that deep tone she found so soothing.

Was there more? Were there to be no secrets from this man? But then, he had the ability to read her soul and she seemed either unable or unwilling to do anything about it. "If you're going to tell me that I'm a very wealthy widow, please don't."

"I wasn't."

She glanced up skeptically. "No?"

His eyes gleamed. "No."

Deanna waited for him to elaborate. When he didn't, she grew impatient. "What *have* you learned about me?"

"You're curious?" His lips twitched at their corners, but having looked back down, she missed the move.

Contrary to her better judgment, Deanna found a demure smile emerging. "I'm a woman. Isn't that one of my prerogatives?"

"*That*'s what I've learned."

"What?" She frowned, puzzled.

Mark grew even more tender, if that were possible, and lifted a hand to press her ear to his heart. "I've learned that you're a woman. Through and through. For every bit of the poise and composure that shields Mrs. Lawrence Hunt from the world, deep down Deanna is a very passionate woman."

She blushed, but he couldn't see that. There was an advantage to sitting this way, she reflected. At least he couldn't see *everything!*

"Well . . . ?" he prodded.

"Well what?"

"Haven't you got anything to say?" She remained silent, feeling almost childish and absurd in light of the very mature experience she and this man had shared. "Nothing?"

"I'm sorry," she finally murmured. "I'm not much of a talker."

Mark was unfazed. "So I gather. And *that's* what I intend to change."

Tilting her head away from his chest, Deanna looked up in good-humored skepticism. "Really?"

"Really." His smile was smug.

"That's very interesting. I've spent nearly thirty years as my own best friend. What makes you think you can change me now?"

He touched her lips with the tip of his finger. "You've been a virgin all that time. . . ." At her cutting glance, he amended his words. "Well . . . almost. Let's say that, for all practical purposes, you were innocent in the ways of passion . . . and I've changed that."

Deanna felt the urge to squirm, but couldn't turn from his riveting warmth. "Was it . . . that obvious?" she asked haltingly.

"Only because I wanted to see it. It was in your eyes and on your lips. When you cried out to me there was an element of . . . I guess you'd call it astonishment."

This time she couldn't hide her blush. "I didn't realize," she breathed self-consciously.

But Mark wasn't finished. His eyes caressed her and she began to tingle with renewed awareness of the hard strength of his body against hers. "You haven't any idea what it meant to me to see that kind of wonder on your face and to know that I'd been able to put it there."

"You're very sure of yourself." She sighed, wishing she possessed even a modicum of that same self-confidence in this very new situation.

"Am I wrong? Have you felt those things before?"

"Please, Mark!" she cried on impulse, desperately needing to put a halt to his prodding. It was getting far too intimate. And despite what they'd just shared, what they continued to share sitting there naked together, she had no desire to discuss her married life. With Larry gone, there was something sacred about those years they'd had together. She wouldn't spoil their memory by discussing very private moments with Mark.

"See, you've said it again. My name." He chuckled at the uncomprehending expression that flitted across her features for a moment.

Deanna took a deep breath. Her eyes broached the subject that her arms and legs weren't quite up to. "I've really got to be going. I do have someone upstairs—a housekeeper. When I left for dinner I told her that I'd be back to do some reading. She's apt to get worried. I don't want her to start making any calls."

"Would she do that?"

"I don't know. I've never given her cause for worry, so she's never been put to the test."

"But she keeps a close watch on you?"

"In the sense of a chaperon . . . no. I'm a big girl." She smiled up at him and was rewarded by a mischievous grin.

"That's what I've been trying to tell you," he drawled, then put his lips to her forehead and pulled her closer for what he sensed would be the final moments of intimacy. "But this housekeeper"—he sobered—"keeps track of your comings and goings?"

"She always knows my schedule so that she can have things ready for me when I need them. It's really very helpful. And after all," she scoffed softly, "it's not as though I run off in odd directions all the time. My life is pretty ordered."

"Ordered . . . or programmed?" He kept his tone a hair above censure.

In its way, Deanna's response was just as pointed, her gaze just as sharp. "Perhaps unchanging, or predictable, would be better choices. There are things to be done on particular days and I do them. I've set a pattern over the years and I don't stray very far. It's a very comfortable, secure way to live."

Mark's eyes didn't leave her face, though the sight of her nudity was his for the taking. He too was preoccupied with this other, more emotional issue. "Is that how you want it?"

Deanna didn't answer for a long time. She had asked herself that same question more than once in the course of the past week. It wasn't a simple matter of "yes" or "no."

"It has been . . ."

"Until now?" Having sensed her hesitancy, Mark probed its cause. But Deanna couldn't confess to him what she refused to confess to herself.

"I don't know. I just don't know." She shook her head, then swung around to take in the room. "This whole thing isn't what I'd planned." Or was it? Was this at the root of the lemon-scented bath she'd taken? Was this behind the black silk and fine pearls? From beneath lowered lids she eyed her delicate bracelet and the matching ring. Those and the strand around her neck were all she wore. She put a hand to her throat.

"I feel so foolish," she whispered, not realizing she'd spoken aloud until Mark turned her around to face him. With only a hand's breadth separating them, she was all too aware of his nakedness. She forced herself to keep her eyes above his waist.

"Why, Deanna? Tell me." He spoke with soft urgency.

Deanna gazed at him achingly as she groped for the words to express her overwhelming confusion. "I . . . everything has always been so clear to me. It's always been so easy. . . ." Her voice trailed off into the silence of the room.

"Go on," Mark coaxed her, gently stroking her arms.

Her brows drew together in a frown. "From as far back as I can remember, my role was cut out for me. I was my parents' daughter, taken care of and protected. I was given everything I could want and more. When it was time to marry, I married. Then Larry took charge of things. The decisions were always made for me by people who knew better than I did. Everything was . . . so simple."

"But there's more to life, Deanna. You've discovered that, haven't you?"

Her eyes grew glazed with a sorrow that boded ill for any future hopes he might have held. "Oh, yes. I've discovered that there's more, but . . ." She felt his hold momentarily slacken and took instant advantage to slide off the bed. With a quick eye to the floor she knelt, gathered her underthings and dress, and stood. Mark was on his feet before her and she gasped in alarm.

If she had thought him intimidating at his full height when dressed, he was that much more so now. In his naked glory he might have been the lean, bronzed hero of every woman's fantasy. His physique was as ideally proportioned as it was superbly conditioned. But he seemed oblivious to his nudity and his eyes refused to release hers to allow her to appreciate him fully.

"But *what?* Say it all," he ordered evenly. This cooler tone was something she hadn't heard from him before and Deanna realized abruptly how very much she didn't know about him. Feeling an instinctive urge to run, she turned toward the bathroom, but he captured her arm and kept her in reach.

"It's not important," she whispered as she clasped her clothes in front of her. Fear erupted within her to join that other swarm of emotions. Could this man who had hitherto shown only gentleness be prone to violence as well? Would the pendulum swing that far?

The sight of her fear gentled him quickly. "It's important to me, Deanna. I've known passion before, but I've never in my life experienced anything like what we had a

little while ago. As a matter of fact, I've never experienced anything like what we've had with that whole
damned dining room separating us! You've felt it. I know
you have. Are you going to turn tail and run from . . .
that?"

The jolt of pain that seared her settled in her chest. It
took the greatest effort she had ever made to say the one
word. "Yes." When Mark looked at her in disbelief, she
tried to explain. "I have to."

"But why?"

If only he *had* been angry, even violent, it might have
been easier for her to do what she had to do. But the total
vulnerability she sensed, the raw anguish of loneliness,
tore into her with a dozen spiked thorns. If this was one of
the things she'd missed in life—the power to hurt—she'd
rather remain in her cocoon.

With a deep breath she began shakily. "I am who I am,
Mark. It's as simple as that . . . and as final." Turning
away, she headed slowly toward the bathroom. "I'm
Mrs. Lawrence Hunt. Certain things are . . . expected of
me." On the threshold she glanced back over her
shoulder. "This isn't one of them." After shutting the
door behind her, she leaned back against it for support,
eyes closed, head back.

Mark had been astonished enough to let her go. But he
soon came to life and strode across the carpet after her.
With his hand on the doorknob he stopped. "But that
isn't fair! You have a right to live."

"I do live," she answered in muffled tones.

The door blunted the full force of his sarcasm. "Oh,
sure. You go through life in very neat progression. *They*
expect . . . and you do. But what about that passion,
Deanna? Why do you have to deny it?"

Deanna started to dress. Her motions held apathy, a
symbol of her need to detach herself from the situation.
Mrs. Lawrence Hunt would never be putting on her

clothes in a strange man's bathroom. Mrs. Lawrence Hunt would never have taken them off in the first place! And as for what had taken place in between—

"Deanna! Answer me!" She heard a muffled oath as he moved away from the door and she sped up in anticipation. Sure enough, she had barely pulled her dress on when the door swung open. Mark had been insightful to the extent of pulling on his slacks, but his manner was in no other way conciliatory. "Okay, honey." He propped his hands on his hips. "You can answer me face-to-face now. I want one good—and I mean *good*—reason why you can't let yourself enjoy life like any other normal person." His eyes glittered with determination. "And don't tell me that you do, because I won't believe it."

With the donning of her clothes, Deanna had moved closer toward being that other woman again. Her poise had finally begun to return. "I'm sorry, Mark, but I can't help that," she apologized softly.

"You can! You can answer me honestly."

"That's what I've been trying to do. But I can't be honest by only giving you the answers you want to hear if those aren't what I *feel*."

Her point was well taken. Mark pondered both it and the beseeching expression on her face. "I know, Deanna." He spoke more gently as he took her hand and led her back through the bedroom to the living room beyond. "But I want you to listen to what I have to say. If you think that tonight has confused *you*, try to consider what *I* feel."

He led her to a small sofa and settled her in the corner before taking a nearby armchair. Leaning forward, he propped his elbows on his knees and clasped his hands together. Deanna saw the lines of concern on his forehead and struggled not to reach out to ease them.

"We met barely a week ago," he began, choosing his

words carefully, as though anguished by his own vulnerability. "There was an instant attraction between us. I
didn't believe it at first, but it persisted until finally I gave
in. Every time our eyes met you spoke to me." He
studied her face for a sign of either rebuke or ridicule.
When he found neither he went on. "When I went back
home I thought of you, remembering how soft you
looked and how . . . open to me. I didn't know your
name then, but I saw how regal you were. It wasn't a total
surprise to learn who you were when I finally mustered
the nerve to ask my waiter."

"You . . . muster the nerve?" Deanna smiled spontaneously. Mark seemed so commanding, with his strong
frame and his compelling air, that for an instant she forgot
that he had unfulfilled needs as well.

"Yes," he grunted back. *"Me* muster the nerve. I felt as
though I was somehow . . . trespassing."

"But that's ridiculous!" she exclaimed.

"Not if you'd been in my place, watching the steady
stream of visitors who obviously knew you and respected
you. *I* was starting from scratch."

Deanna sobered at his reference to her life as Mrs.
Hunt. Had that been a lure for him? Could he have been
attracted by her status? It was feasible to imagine that she
could be exploited. Was that what he wanted to do?

When he spoke again she found her fears dissolving.
"You know, I half wish that you were a struggling working
girl. It would be very easy for me to sweep you off your
feet. I could offer you all those things you've never had
and bowl you over with my worldliness." He laughed in
self-mockery and shook his head sadly. "But you're not a
struggling working girl, are you? You've got everything
money can buy. I can only offer you"—his voice lowered
—"those things that aren't for sale. Those things that
can't be priced."

Deanna sat raptly, listening to him, her gaze captured.

At the last heartfelt declaration she felt the prick of tears in her eyes. Looking down in vain denial of the emotion he stirred, she tried to focus on his words, but those to come were even more emotion-laden.

"You came to me willingly tonight, didn't you?" he asked pointedly.

She twisted the pearl ring slowly on her finger as she struggled to recall its origin. But the fact that it had been a gift from Larry was suddenly irrelevant. "Yes," she whispered, unable to lie.

"Why, Deanna? Why did you come? Why did you let me make love to you?"

She shrugged, frowned and stared at his hands. They were strong and warm and she wished one held her own hand. She recalled how gently he'd touched her, how sweetly he'd caressed her body and brought her to the moment of fulfillment she'd never experienced before. Soft tremors tickled her insides in memory of that glorious instant. But it was past. Now she was being asked to examine her motives. How did one bare one's soul when its contents were an enigma?

Her eyes fell on her own hands, clutched together with tension. "Don't ask me to explain myself," she pleaded softly. "I don't think I can do that."

"Can you see me again . . . tomorrow night?"

Her head flew up. "No."

Though he'd known what the answer would be, it was no easier to accept. "You haven't got other plans, have you?" Silently she shook her head, then raised her brows as he continued. "Will you tell me something, Deanna?" She waited. "Have there been other men since your husband died?"

Startled by his directness, she stiffened. "You don't need me to answer that, do you?"

Mark's chuckle held admiration. "The perfect evasion."

"I didn't mean it that way," she put in quickly. "But I'm sure you already know the answer. If I'd been with other men I would be taking this all in stride rather than agonizing over it, wouldn't I?"

"It's possible"—he arched a brow—"that what you felt with me was powerful enough to frighten you." The ensuing pause was pregnant with meaning. "Well . . . ?"

Deanna jumped to her feet. "I've got to go. Really."

"You can't!" Mark stood up just as quickly and reached out to feather-touch the auburn silk of her hair. "I mean . . ." He shifted self-consciously, grinned sheepishly, then broke into an exquisitely tender smile. "That is . . . you'd better hitch up your hair again. It looks positively beautiful to me . . . but that housekeeper of yours is apt to wonder."

Deanna put a hand to her shoulder, where her tresses spilled in sensual luxury. "Oh!" she gasped, then blushed, even dared to laugh at herself. "I forgot! You're right. She would wonder . . ."

"Come on." He tilted his head. "You can use my things."

Unwilling to argue, she felt characteristically docile as she retraced her steps to the bathroom. Mark fished a brush from his leather kit, handed it to her, then leaned back against the doorjamb to watch her work.

After several long strokes she paused. "My hair will be all over your brush. . . ."

He crossed his arms over his chest and beamed in delight at the sight before him. "I don't mind. Except for the length, it'd be hard to tell your hair from mine. And it's not as if I have a jealous wife to wonder who's been sharing my hairbrush."

Deanna froze. Unable to move, she stared at Mark in the mirror. "You *don't* have one, do you?" she asked, horrified at the thought of what she might have done. Indeed, much of her horror was due to the fact that the possibility of his being married hadn't once entered her mind.

But rather than ridiculing her naiveté as he might have done, Mark laughed his pleasure and shook his head in gentle wonder. "No, honey. I'm not married. If I was I would never have invited you here tonight. I might have sentenced myself to a hell of frustration, but I wouldn't have made love to you. I do have *some* scruples."

Hiding her relief with a renewed assault on her hair, Deanna turned to silently scrutinize her own image. She had given herself to a man tonight and she barely knew him. What did that say about *her* values? What did it say about her past . . . her future? Who was he really? Had he ever been married? And what was he doing in Atlanta?

Mark grinned knowingly. "Okay, Ms. Hunt. Is there something else you'd like to ask?"

"No!" she vowed softly.

"You're sure? I thought you'd be curious."

She found no amusement in his own apparent amusement. Perhaps that was what hardened her. "The less I know, the easier it will be . . ."

She'd hit her mark. His features sobered instantly. "To walk out on me?"

Grimacing, she softened. "It's not quite that way."

"But that *is* the end effect," he countered quietly.

Holding her hair up with one hand, Deanna blushed to realize that her silk clips were back on the bed where they'd fallen in the storm of passion. Mark produced them magically from his pocket.

"I'd like to see you again," he persisted.

She felt the spark of his touch when he calmly handed the clips to her and she tried to dispel its searing effect by fiddling with her hair.

"That's not possible." With a few deft tucks her hair was acceptably secured. Determined to leave, she turned from the mirror. But Mark filled the doorway, hand posted on either side of the frame. "Please," she begged. "It's very late. I'll be missed."

"First . . . a kiss." He stood firm, unwavering.

"Mark . . . please . . ."

"A kiss."

Her shoulders sagged under the weight of frustration. Lifting a hand, she rubbed at the tension above her eyes. "Why? There's no point. What would it accomplish?"

His lips twitched in humor. "Why don't we see?"

She should have taken warning at his sureness, but there were too many emotions warring in her mind to allow for clear thought. "Let me go," she whispered in a final plea as she gazed the wistful distance up at him.

"One kiss," he teased with precise enunciation, his smile gently masculine and insistent.

"Mark . . ."

"One!"

Deanna sensed that he wouldn't release her until she'd complied with what seemed on the surface to be such a simple request. She felt her own growing agony and knew that she had to get away soon. His closeness was a bittersweet torment.

Mindful only of her need to escape, she stepped close, tipped her head up and put her lips tentatively to his. Therein lay the catch. He hadn't moved. He still filled the doorway, blocking her flight. Only his lips moved . . . but with devastating effect.

It was as though Deanna were being given one final glimpse of the heaven she'd sampled earlier. At her first timid touch Mark's lips began a sweet caress that blossomed to tantalize her with its honey. It coaxed and tasted, savored and revered until it had successfully extracted Deanna's unconscious sigh of capitulation.

Quite without knowing it, she slid her arms about his waist to the warm, vibrantly muscular span of his back and returned his kiss with the same poignant need it had itself demonstrated. She knew only the mindless pleasure she felt—the comfort, the warmth, the delicious languor seeping slowly through her. When Mark finally dragged his head up and set her back, she was breathless.

"Well?" he croaked, breathing heavily himself. *"Did* it accomplish anything?" His brown eyes glowed as she knew hers must have done.

But she couldn't speak. Her throat was choked with emotions ranging from confusion, panic and despair to hope. Had this final kiss accomplished anything? Oh, yes, it certainly had. It had reminded her of how special Mark was, how unique their relationship, how very priceless that which they had shared. Hadn't he said it himself . . . that he could only offer her what money couldn't buy? Well, she reflected with mounting anguish, he had offered it to her. Now it was her duty to refuse the gift.

The shakiness of her limbs was no obstacle to what she knew to be her own responsibility. Drawing herself up straighter she devoured his handsome features for a last moment, then took a deep, sorrowful breath. "It's convinced me that I was wrong to have come here in the first place, Mark." Before her aching gaze his face grew pained. "You have to understand that my life is . . . my life. I can't change it. Not yet, at least. I'm not, . . . ready. This is too new. There's too much to consider."

"But you came here tonight—"

"It was a lapse!" she cried, finding a hidden reserve of strength to push past him and hurry through the suite.

"But it reflected a deep need!" He followed her, his voice rising, though well controlled.

"No!" She turned to him, then away. She realized that this forceful denial of his claim might be less than honest. Ashamed and frightened, she couldn't look back again. "No! I'm fine." She drew open the door of the suite, moved through and closed it behind herself without knowing that Mark had stopped at the edge of the bedroom to watch her departure with rigidly enforced dignity.

"I'm fine," she whispered softly, willing her tears not to fall as she mustered her own waning dignity and approached the elevator.

# 4

The tears could only be held back so long. Deanna remained dry-eyed and composed through the short trip to the fortieth floor. She calmly let herself into her suite, answered Irma's questions with the remarkably firm assurance that she'd had a pleasant evening, then retreated at last to the privacy of her own room. There she sank down onto the softness of the cushioned lounge and cried.

Even Larry's death hadn't prompted so anguished a flood of tears. Then she had known a grief bounded by the finality of death. What one couldn't change, one had to accept. This situation was different.

As the sleepless hours passed and her tears slowly dried, she tried to assimilate what had happened, tried to find a proper perspective with which to view it. But she couldn't. Everywhere she looked she saw evidence of the life she'd lived for what seemed like forever. There in the bedroom she'd shared with Larry she could find no room at all for fantasy.

She finally slept for several hours before awakening, groggy and unsure, to the buzz of her alarm. Though a hot bath eased the dismaying tautness in her thighs, nothing could ease the unsettled state of her mind. She was sure of only one thing: She had no desire to face Mark Birmingham in the hotel dining room that morning. Her feelings were far too raw and he read them far too accurately. It would take time for her to fully restore the veneer of composure that was such a vital part of her image.

Unfortunately, Mark had no intention of granting her that time. She was sitting at her dressing table, taking her frustration out on her thick mane of hair, when the muffled sound of the doorbell reached her. She knew who it was instantly. Putting her brush down slowly, she stared at her reflection until the soft knock on her door drew her gaze in that direction.

"Yes, Irma?"

The housekeeper timidly eased the door open. Her voice was quieter than usual and distinctly hesitant. "Excuse me, Mrs. Hunt, but there's a Mr. Birmingham to see you. I've explained that you weren't up yet, but he's quite insistent. He says that you'd arranged to meet him for breakfast."

*The rogue!* Deanna stiffened, but forced herself to hear Irma out without interrupting.

"He was worried when you were late." Irma paused. "And so am I." Her plea grew more personal. "Are you feeling all right?"

Deanna took a deep breath, only then making her decision. "I'm fine. Just tired. I thought I'd have some coffee here this morning."

For a few seconds the two women eyed one another expectantly. Irma finally broke the ice. "And Mr. Birmingham? Shall I tell him that you're unable to see him now?" Her own feelings on the matter were well hidden.

Deanna turned back to the mirror and gripped her brush fiercely. "No. Tell him I'll be right out." Before she could change her mind Irma had left to deliver the message. And it was just as well. Procrastination was only a stopgap measure. If the man was persistent enough to appear at her door, an immediate confrontation was called for. Cowardice had no place here. She refused to become a prisoner in her own hotel out of fear of bumping into Mark Birmingham!

With a bolstering surge of indignation Deanna tugged the tie of her silk robe more tightly, left the sanctuary of her room and made the silent journey down the hall toward the foyer. But Mark was already in the living room, his back to her, his eyes on the jagged skyline of Atlanta.

She stood for a bit watching him, calmly accepting his tall, lean form, dark-suited and very proper once more. She told herself that he really wasn't that much different from other men. But then he turned and shattered that wish.

He didn't say anything at first, simply stared at her across her exquisitely decorated living room. There weren't any people to separate them now or to ensure the propriety of their interchange. Even so, neither moved toward the other. Deanna wasn't the only one with a face full of emotion.

He looked tired. She thought she saw the same vulnerability, the same need and curiosity, but it was hard to tell through the very definite anger there. She knew a moment's fear at the fact that this man whom she barely knew could so easily betray her. She had given him the weapon herself. Would he use it?

"Deanna?" He hesitated. "Can we talk?"

He seemed so dark in contrast to the cream coloring of

the room that she felt momentarily strong. The fantasy was incongruous in this setting. He was out of his element. In this Hunt stronghold she was safe.

Nodding, she gestured politely toward the sofa. "Would you . . . like to sit down?" He was too imposing, stronghold or no. Setting an example for him to follow, she eased down into a corner of the couch, but Mark wasn't her usual guest and had no intention of following her polite courtesies. He chose to stand and, in so doing, only exaggerated the height discrepancy she'd sought to diminish.

Sighing, Deanna focused on her hands. Again there was a decision to be made. She could skirt the issue . . . or hit home. She chose the latter and faced him defiantly. "Irma said that you'd expected me for breakfast. You had no right to tell her that."

"She looked so wary of me that I had to think up some reasonable excuse for appearing here so early. It was the first one that came to mind." His gaze narrowed in speculation. "You really don't have many suitors, do you?"

She tipped her chin up a notch. "I'm not in the market for a companion." The word was inappropriate and brought a sly grin to Mark's face.

"No, it certainly wasn't a companion you were looking for last night." Was he mocking her?

"Mark . . . please . . ."

But her quiet warning went unheeded. The pleasantness in his tone couldn't deny his determination any more than the dark glitter in his eyes could. "You needed something and I gave it to you. I needed something and *you* gave it to *me*. It went far beyond . . . companionship." He stood with his legs apart, his hands in his pants pockets. Had Deanna not been shrouded in her own emotional turmoil she might have been intimidated.

But she bolted from her seat to stand before him, matching his purposefulness with a will of her own. "What do you want, Mark?"

"You."

"I'm not available."

"I think you are."

It was a standoff, and driven by desperation, Deanna wasn't about to back down first. "It doesn't matter what you think. There can't be any kind of relationship without two willing partners." No sooner had the words left her mouth than she regretted them.

Mark seized on them quickly. "You were willing enough last night."

"I told you, that was a lapse," she countered just as quickly, wanting only to lessen the humiliation she felt. "It was a mistake. I shouldn't have gone with you. And you shouldn't be here." She glared at him with her last bit of strength before retreating to the window. Atlanta was Lawrence Hunt's town. It seemed critical to remember that. But how could she concentrate when Mark approached? Even without turning, she felt his nearness.

"Look, Deanna," he began, then halted abruptly enough that she looked around. To her dismay, Irma was calmly setting down a tray bearing juice, muffins and coffee—more than enough for two. Had the woman chanced a look at her mistress she might have felt the silent chastisement Deanna cast her way. But Irma had both a thick shell and a strong sense of purpose herself. She made her exit without a word being spoken.

"A-hah!" Mark crowed softly, drawing Deanna's crestfallen face toward him once more. "It's good to know that *someone* is looking out for my welfare this morning." With a smile and an infuriatingly nonchalant step he crossed to the side table, poured two cups of coffee and handed one to Deanna, but only after he'd sternly pointed to the sofa and she'd meekly sat.

But her meekness was surface deep. "You mean to say that you didn't even eat breakfast while you were waiting downstairs?" she asked as she grasped at the last of her poise. Mark's nearness made things so difficult.

"I didn't even bother to take a table. Since I'd half suspected you'd skip out on me, I waited in the lobby for five or ten minutes before heading up here."

"That was presumptuous of you," she gritted. "I thought I'd made my feelings clear last night."

"You did." He grinned. "Perfectly."

"That's not what I meant and you know it, Mark! We have no future. There was no sense in your coming here."

Having sunk to the sofa, Mark very deliberately reached across her to the tray. He had to know that she felt his warmth, that her senses reacted instinctively to the tang of his after-shave and his manly freshness.

"Muffin?" he asked sweetly.

"No!"

His sidelong glance caught her blush. "You're sure? You have to be hungry . . ."

*After last night?* "I'm not," she snapped. "You do strange things to my appetite."

"That's funny. I was thinking the same thing about you earlier. I can't begin to tell you what I ate for dinner last night."

She'd had that experience herself and he knew it. With a loud sigh and the clatter of her coffee cup as she set it on the side table, Deanna acknowledged defeat. She wasn't skilled at this sparring. She'd never had to do it. Nothing in her life had prepared her for psychological warfare.

With her elbows on her knees and her fingertips against her brow, she spoke sadly. "Go away, Mark. Don't you see—I'm not up for this. What happened last night shouldn't have! It can't happen again! I'm my husband's wife—"

"Widow! He's dead, Deanna!"

Her gaze shot up, her eyes filled with tears. *"Don't you think I know that?"* she cried loudly, bringing Irma scurrying from the kitchen. It was only Mark's upraised hand and faint headshake that held her off, then sent her away with the assurance that Deanna was all right.

Oblivious to the near intrusion, Deanna had burrowed into the corner of the sofa. Though her tears remained unshed, her misery was evident.

"Do you miss him badly?" Mark asked. His voice was suddenly much softer and so gentle that she couldn't resist him. Here was a glimpse of her soulmate again. He seemed to want to know her feelings as much as she needed to tell them. It had all been held in for so long.

Arms wrapped protectively around her middle, Deanna slowly perused the room. "Yes, I miss him. In so many ways he was my world. It revolved around him."

"You depended on him." The statement brought a frown to Deanna's face.

"Uh-huh," she whispered. "I did."

"How long has he been gone?"

She sighed, eyes glued to the pink folds of her silk robe. "Fourteen months now."

"You can't still be in mourning?" When she looked up sharply to counter his criticism, he qualified it. "Wait! That came out all wrong. I'm just trying to understand why you won't see me. You're a young woman. You can't bury yourself here forever." He skimmed the suite before adding a low-murmured, "lovely as this place is."

But Deanna had grown more fearful by the minute and was beyond noticing the compliment. He was such an attractive man. Her senses sharpened even against her will. "What is it you want, Mark?" she asked, using bluntness as a means of self-control. "Is it strictly a matter of a . . . bedmate?"

"You know it's not!" he exploded in a burst of frustration. "If it was simply a matter of sex I wouldn't be here now. No man likes to invite rejection."

All too aware of his hurt, she softened. "Then what is it? Why *me?*" Perhaps her own ego needed boosting as well.

When she looked up beseechingly, Mark captured her gaze. His eyes held that vulnerability to which she was herself so vulnerable and the now-familiar warmth came to life. She knew his answer before he gave it, though his grudging admission took her by surprise. It was as though he resented the power that rendered him help-less, regardless of its source. He was a strong man. This confession was a difficult one.

"*You,* Deanna, because you're special. You have something that I've never found in another woman. What? I don't think I can put it into words yet, but I do know what I want . . . I *need* someone. Emotionally as well as physically. You need the same thing. I can tell." She shook her head in denial, but her inner responses had already made a mockery of it. "I'm not sorry about what happened last night," he continued, "only that it happened so quickly that it frightened you." He paused to study her pale face, the haunted sheen of her eyes. "Can't we start over again? More slowly this time?"

It was a deep-seated fear, enigmatic but pure, that brought her from the sofa. "No, Mark. I can't. I told you last night—my life is already cut out for me. I can't change it." She inhaled and felt the shooting pain of regret.

"Can't?" He was on his feet, towering before her, suddenly less patient. "That's absurd! You can do what-ever you want! *You* . . . of *all* people! You're a free woman!"

"Freedom is relative. I have freedom—"

"Within limits. Is that it?" he asked, echoing her own soul-searching. "But what about you? Forget the Hunt Corporation. Forget the Hunt Foundation. Forget the world Lawrence Hunt bequeathed you. What about *you*? What about *your* freedom?"

She had no answers and trembled under the strain. "I think you ought to leave."

Mark stepped closer. "Not until you agree to see me again."

Her eye fell to the pulse throbbing at his neck and her own accelerated. "I won't. I told you . . . I'm not ready!"

"Oh, you're ready." He moved closer, until he was only a breath away.

Deanna couldn't move. There was nothing of the fantasy in this room that was so thoroughly Hunt, so completely reality. Yet she was frozen in place, immobilized by the same physical force that had possessed her the night before. "No," she whispered, shaking her head slowly. "No . . ."

The word was meant as much for herself as for him and had no effect on either of them. When he reached out to touch her lips she ached to respond. It had been so sweet before. Would it be as much so a second time?

"Try," he murmured, reading her thoughts. Then he dipped his head to taste her lips in a string of feather-light kisses that tormented her with maddening evasion.

Closing her eyes to blot out reality, she welcomed fantasy with the parting of her lips. But it was to be a game. Mark's teasing mouth captured hers, then darted away before she could claim satisfaction. When she could stand no more she cried aloud, a small cry representing an anguish far greater than the physical frustration she felt. The unexpected sound startled her. Her eyes flew open and reality returned.

Her cry this time was more akin to despair. Jerking

back as though burned by fire rather than desire, she clamped a fist to her mouth, stared at Mark in horror for a last minute, then fled down the hall in confusion.

Somehow she knew he wouldn't follow. Even he wouldn't be so crass as to invade the bedroom she'd shared for so many years with Larry. But her mind was not on Larry as she collapsed onto the lounge and hugged her knees to her chest. What was she going to do with Mark?

Not for a minute did she believe that this would be the end of it. The light in his eyes had been far too intense. It was simply a question of when he would next make a move. She couldn't stay in the sanctuary of her bedroom forever.

As she dressed to go to the club she struggled to sort through her thoughts, but her emotions were diverse and in conflict with one another. She felt shame at her abandonment of the night before amid a lingering excitement. She felt guilt at her indulgence even as her insides cried for more. She felt a fear she didn't understand and a mourning for that passing fantasy. And, against her better judgment, she was still curious. Who *was* Mark Birmingham and why was he in Atlanta?

It was Thursday. She'd held herself to her routine as a means of self-preservation, even daring to breakfast in the dining room that morning. But even without looking toward the window, she knew that Mark wasn't there. She would have felt his presence. Instead she felt the emptiness of a fantasy gone awry and she couldn't help but acknowledge a mild regret. Mark had been right—that she knew. She *did* need something—someone—in her life. What they'd shared the other night—its beauty, its exhilaration, its marvelous sense of fulfillment—had convinced her of that. Yet she was frightened and confused and so very, very unsure that she could only be grateful for the time without him.

That afternoon, however, she had no more than set foot into Bob Warner's office when she sensed something new.

"How are you, Deanna?" Bob had risen from his desk to greet her before she'd had time to cross the room herself.

"Fine, Bob. How are things here?"

"Not bad." He grinned, a trifle too smugly for her comfort.

"Uh-oh. Something's up."

Bob took her elbow. "Come on. Let's take a walk. I want you to see the plans."

"The plans? For the hospital?" She perked up, temporarily willing to ignore the prickling under her skin as she fell into step beside him.

"That's right."

"But I thought we were still getting bids. . . ."

"No, ma'am. We're still trying to figure out how to raise the rest of the money, but the decision on the firm was made last week."

Deanna eyed him sharply. "Why wasn't I told?"

Unfazed by her disturbance, he seemed happy to treat it as he would a child's show of temper. "A surprise, Deanna." He grinned again. "Come on. I've purposely waited until there was something for you to see."

Turning a corner, he propelled her toward one of the smaller conference rooms, opened its door, then stood back to let her enter. The instant she saw the tall figure she knew. The pieces of the puzzle—some of them, at least—suddenly fit together. He stood at one side of the long conference table, bending over it to make notations on one of the many blueprints spread before him. His jacket was off, his shirt-sleeves rolled to the elbow. He looked devilishly handsome even before his dark head swung up to acknowledge the intrusion.

"I hope we're not disturbing you, Mark." Bob's voice came from directly behind Deanna to snap her from her paralysis as his hand guided her forward. "Deanna, I'd like you to meet Mark Birmingham. His architectural firm has just completed the preliminary design for the hospital. Mark . . . Deanna Hunt."

For a brief moment Deanna knew an awesome terror. It shimmered in her eyes, which never left Mark's. Would he betray her? Would he hint at their relationship? Would he embarrass her in front of Bob? Thanks to her foolishness he had the tool. . . .

But his expression was one of absolute composure. It held neither gloating nor smugness. As his gaze shifted slowly from Bob to her, he smiled so innocently that he might have been meeting her for the first time. "Mrs. Hunt." He straightened and stepped forward to extend his hand. "It's a pleasure to meet you."

Weak-kneed with relief, she returned the smile and offered her hand in return. Though his touch sizzled through her skin and into her bloodstream, she clutched at his show of silence as a timely salvation.

"Mr. Birmingham . . ." She nodded her head, rising to the occasion with studied poise. "Congratulations on having won the hospital contract. And welcome to the Hunt Foundation." How she managed to remain as cool as she did, she'd never know. But she accepted his nod of response graciously.

"Mark is with the firm of—"

"Birmingham and Swift, I believe," Deanna interrupted, startling both herself and Bob with her forwardness. "You're headquartered in Savannah, aren't you, Mr. Birmingham?"

The eyes before her suddenly danced. "That's right. But it's 'Mark.' Please."

As she donned her most charming smile she determined that this demon would not get the best of her. Two could play at this game as well as one. And though she resented Bob for having excluded her from the decision-making process, it was a *fait accompli*. Mark Birmingham would be designing her hospital! It would take some getting used to, having him here . . . but it seemed she had no choice.

"Tell me, Mr. Birmingham—uh, Mark," she corrected herself, "have you ever done anything on this scale before? I've heard of your firm"—though she didn't say where or when—"but I know nothing about your work."

Bob's voice was a subtle reminder that she and Mark weren't alone. As Deanna tore her gaze from Mark's she realized that she'd been staring. It was one of the things she'd have to watch.

"Mark's firm established itself doing business complexes and shopping malls. Lately he's done more work for educational institutions. He designed the state university's new library last year and I understand that the art museum of his in West Virginia has brought in raves. This is your first hospital though, isn't it, Mark?"

Mark leaned back against the edge of the table and folded his arms across his chest. "First one." At his grin, Deanna reacted on impulse.

"You seem pretty pleased with yourself." She stood on tiptoe and tried to steal a glance at the prints behind him. "Is that why you're hiding your blueprints from me?" she teased.

He dropped his complacency with a thoroughly endearing abruptness. "Oh! That's right. Here, take a look and tell me what you think."

If she thought she'd caught him off guard, Deanna had underestimated the opposition. He knew precisely what he was doing as he stood aside to let her examine the tableful of prints. She looked carefully from one sheet to the other, searching for something of meaning to her among the myriad lines and figures. After her show of savvy in naming Mark's firm, she felt particularly stupid now. Worse, Mark was enjoying her discomfort.

"Well?" he prodded. "Are you impressed?"

"Very," she replied with a wry twist to her lips. "You must be brilliant to have drawn up these papers. But they're meaningless to me." She dared to look up. "Perhaps you'd tell me what I'm looking at?"

If Bob was aware of her soft sarcasm or the silent current coursing between Mark and herself, he ignored it. Mark, on the other hand, was impressed with her forthrightness and took instant pity on her.

"Here." He reached forward to extract several large sheets from the bottom of the pile. "I think these are more along the line of what you'd expected."

They were . . . and they weren't. Before her were a series of ink sketches of the proposed design, drawings of what the finished hospital would look like. This Deanna could appreciate. What she hadn't anticipated was the stunning effect Mark had created by taking traditional structural elements and giving them excitingly modern interpretations. It was indeed a hospital, but like no other she'd ever seen.

"Well . . . ?" This time his urging was sober and earnest; he was obviously on edge with anticipation.

But before Deanna could respond the telephone buzzed. Had she not been positively enchanted by the sketches before her she might have lent an ear to Bob's low conversation and been better prepared for his departure, even ready with an excuse to leave with him. Being left alone in the room with Mark was not what she wanted. Unfortunately, she was left with no option.

Bob turned to them on his way toward the door. "You'll have to excuse me for a few minutes. I've been waiting for this overseas call too long to ignore it. I'll be back." Then he was gone, leaving the door ajar.

Mark sauntered over and closed it without pretense. Then he turned to Deanna, leaned back against the door, put his hands in his pockets and smiled. "Well. Here we are."

All else was temporarily forgotten but the two of them. Deanna had known how to handle herself skillfully moments earlier; now she was breaking new ground. "You knew all along, didn't you, Mark?"

He arched one brow. "That I'd be designing your hospital? Not until last Friday when I got Bob's call. But I didn't learn who *you* were until Tuesday morning. Quite a coincidence, I'd say."

"I'm sure you would," she muttered, turning away in impotence. She felt so helpless and she was tired of it.

"You're not angry, are you?" He had approached to stand by her side, looking down at her.

"At you?" She glanced up to meet his gaze. "No. At the situation . . . yes."

He cocked his head toward the door. "Does he walk out and leave you to the wolves like this often?"

Deanna snickered at his interpretation of her words. "He has this way of conveniently unloading me on whomever he can corral to keep me busy. But you've received the supreme compliment. He must trust you."

"And you?" His lids lowered heavily. "Do you trust me?"

Deanna had no wish to answer his question. With a deep breath she turned back to the table. "As an architect, you're unbelievable. These sketches are magnificent!"

She felt the warmth of his breath against her cheek as he leaned over her shoulder to share the view. "I'm glad you like them," he whispered, then kissed her neck so softly that she might have believed she'd imagined it, had not his tongue offered an erotic follow-up that in turn made her shiver.

"Mark!" she gasped, jumping away. "No, I don't trust you! Alone in a room . . . not for a minute!" Nor did she trust herself; the deep internal ache had begun again. She didn't know whether to swallow her pride and flee or try to fend him off until Bob returned. "You know, you're as bad as Bob is."

Mark frowned. "How so?"

"You might have told me about this"—she gestured broadly toward the table—"the other night."

"As I recall, you didn't want to know anything about me. I offered." He had indeed, she had to admit.

"But this was something I *should* have known about."

"Before . . . or after?"

"Either!"

"Would it have made a difference?" he asked, beginning to gather the plans into a large pile. "Would you *not* have come upstairs with me had you known beforehand that I'd be doing work for your foundation?"

Instead of answering, Deanna wandered to the far end of the table and eased down into the black leather chair at its head. With her arms propped on its wooden ones, she crossed her legs and tried to feel comfortable. It was impossible. The whir of her emotions continued to disturb her.

"Tell me, Deanna, would you have done differently had you known?"

He had come to stand directly before her and she had to tip her head back to meet his gaze. "Yes. I would never have gone with you."

A low breath passed his lips. "You're pretty sure about that. How about the reason behind it?"

She looked down, hesitant. Her reasoning was clear to her, but could she express it to another? "I don't know,

Mark." She sighed. "What happened between us was
. . . unreal. Had I identified you with the foundation I
couldn't have gone through with it. I would have been
. . . frightened."

"Of scandal?"

He hit the mark. "I suppose you could call it that."

"Are you afraid now?" he asked gently, tilting her chin
up with his finger.

Deanna had only to look at him for a minute to feel a
surge of desire. "Yes," she whispered. Her lower lip
trembled; her eyes glowed with a need she wanted to
ignore.

Releasing her chin with a caress, he leaned over to
place an arm on either side of hers, bringing his head
down close by her face. "Can you tell me about it,
Deanna? Tell me what frightens you."

"You're asking a lot."

"You've done well so far. Why not keep trying?"

He was so different, she mused. No one had ever
coaxed her to reveal herself like this. He was special. She
wanted nothing more than to touch him. Instead she
clenched her fists and averted her gaze, but he seemed to
be everywhere . . . large, clean, strong. His pale blue
shirt covered broad muscles; his gray slacks stretched
across unending legs. She found herself wondering what
color briefs were beneath those slacks, then stifled a gasp.

His nearness had stripped her of her protective veneer
until her words held only the truth. "I'm frightened of so
many things—things that I don't understand. Yes, scandal
has to be one. I wouldn't want to do anything to hurt the
foundation or its work."

"Do you think that *I* would?" he asked in a murmur.

Deanna shrugged. "I don't know."

"I didn't let on anything to Warner, did I?"

"No."

"See? Don't you think that merits some degree of

trust?" His voice did wild things to her insides; his closeness did even more wicked things to her senses.

There was desperation in her gaze when she raised it to his. "I want to trust you, Mark. But I don't know you."

"And that's what I'm trying to change," he vowed, but she barely heard him because his lips were far too near for rational thought. She was mesmerized and stared at them until they moved to breathe her name. "Deanna . . ." Then they lowered to kiss her and reason began to recede.

All sense of place and purpose was lost in the silent cry that echoed between them. Mark's lips parted hers with a gentleness that melted her resistance with a single taste. She was once more yielding to passion's fantasy and it was as mind-bending as before.

"Oh, Mark." She sighed when he released her lips to draw her from the chair and into his full embrace. His body was tall, sturdy and beckoning. When he leaned against the edge of the table he tucked her between his thighs. Then he kissed her again.

Deanna couldn't imagine anything as beautiful as the sense of participation, of giving, she felt at the movement of her lips on his and the slow circling of her arms to his neck. Her body fitted against him perfectly as her hands molded the vibrancy of his sinewed shoulders.

"See what we've got," he whispered against her neck. "It's so natural and real."

But it wasn't. Not in Deanna's mind. She was once more transported by fantasy, willing every bit of worry and confusion into oblivion. He could do this to her— drive everything from mind but the need to satisfy him. And she found her body craving more.

With a breathy moan she tipped her head to the side. Mark's lips warmed her neck as she murmured his name. Restlessness possessed her and she moved against him. It seemed that her only true fulfillment was in this man's arms. He made her something unique. She'd never felt as needed as when he pressed her closer and poignantly outlined his rising desire.

When he framed her face once more he concentrated on her lips, consuming their sweet offering with a growing hunger. Her own hunger was no less. The hands that had fallen to his thighs for support now found another purpose. Her fingers splayed there broadly, gliding upward over his tautness. She felt him stiffen further and gloried in her power.

"Feel good?" He nibbled at her lips.

"Mmmmmm." She sighed. "You always feel good. How do you do it?"

"I'm a man. Made for you. Just as you're made for me."

She looked up at him then and her body ached. He must have read her pain, because he let his hands trail from her neck to her shoulders, then down to her breasts. She breathed in deeply and swelled to his touch, but she wanted more, so much more.

Her smooth silk blouse and the sheer bra beneath were no barrier to his questing fingers, which found her nipples unerringly and caressed them until he felt them peak. She could only moan and close her eyes as she wondered if the delicious torment would ever end. She desperately wanted it to . . . but only if it led to more intimate caresses.

"See what you've done to me?" she cried softly and he hugged her tightly in response.

"Tell me."

"You've made me want you so badly that I can't think straight."

"That's only fair, considering what *you've* done to *me.*"

"And what's that?" she whispered against his chest, hearing the jagged leap of his heart, a herald of his confession. But his voice was so suddenly sober that she pulled back to look at him. His eyes were the richest shade of brown she'd ever seen.

"You've made everything else seem insignificant. The work that means so much to me suddenly doesn't. It's behind me on this table and I couldn't care less. All I care about at this minute is holding you, kissing you, making love to you. . . ."

Deanna shared the feeling. Though she couldn't bring herself to say them, her eyes echoed his words.

Mark grew suddenly troubled and set her gently away from him. "The worst of it is that I forget myself, Deanna. This is Hunt territory. What we're doing here will only complicate your worries. Not that I agree with them, mind you. You have nothing to fear from me. I wouldn't do anything to jeopardize your position. But you're worried about something, aren't you?"

Slowly recovering from the passionate high she'd been on moments earlier, Deanna stared at Mark, then looked away. With this return of reality had come a spate of worries, but they weren't at all those she'd expected. Distracted, she turned and wandered the length of the conference table, finally stopping just beyond the sketches of the proposed hospital.

"It's really beautiful, Mark," she complimented him softly. "I'm glad you're doing this for us."

He opened his mouth to say something, then changed his mind when a sound at the door drew their attention.

"Sorry about that!" Bob burst through the door, totally oblivious to what he'd missed. "It took longer than I'd thought." Pausing, he looked expectantly from Deanna to Mark and back. "Well, Deanna? Do we have your approval?"

*Did you ever really need it?* she asked silently, but forced an outward return to character. "It's perfect, Bob.

You chose the architect well. Our hospital will be the pride of Atlanta."

"I knew you'd think so! But now PR is waiting for you. Shall we go?"

With a docile nod Deanna started for the door. Then she paused. "I know the way, Bob. Surely you have something more urgent . . . ?"

Bob managed to cover his surprise with a downward glance at his watch. "I do have an appointment at Emory regarding those fellowships," he mused aloud, then looked up. "Are you all set here, Mark?"

Mark swung his head toward the stack of blueprints. "I'd like to go over these once more before I leave. Do you mind if I use this room a little longer?"

"Of course not. Take your time. You'll be back on Tuesday?"

Deanna's ears perked up. So he was returning to Savannah and would be away over the weekend. That must have been his pattern the week before too.

Mark saw her comprehension before he answered Bob. "That's right. Next week should do it on the preliminaries."

Only Bob seemed pleased. "Good work! Then it will be up to us to finish raising the money. Think we can do it, Deanna?"

It took her a minute to ingest his question. "Uh, I think so. We'll certainly try." She hesitated, wanting . . . not wanting. "Well, I'd better get downstairs."

"And I'd better be on my way. Deanna, I'll talk with you tomorrow. Mark, see you Tuesday."

As she stood by and watched the two men shake hands, she felt suspended, waiting for a final word she had no right to. Then, with a soft-spoken "Mark . . ." and a parting nod, she left the conference room. Her steps were unusually slow and lingering, while Bob

Warner went in the opposite direction at a more business-like clip.

Head down she waited . . . wondering. When she stopped and dared to look back, the hall was empty . . . except for Mark's tall frame propped against the doorway of the room she'd just left. In that split second, as her hopes took flight, Deanna knew that she had crossed a threshold of sorts. It only remained to determine exactly where she'd go from there.

# 5

~~~~~~~~~~

She stood still, watching him silently. When he made no move to step forward she understood that the decision was hers. Trying to ignore the knots that had suddenly bunched in her stomach, she retraced her steps until she faced him.

But words failed her. She had no idea what she wanted to say, given the overwhelming confusion she felt. Mark waited patiently, reading the war of emotions in her troubled gaze. Finally, feeling dreadfully inadequate, she forced herself to speak. The best she could do was a soft and faltering murmur. "Mark . . . I don't know what to say . . . uh . . . I'm not really sure . . ."

His finger touched her lips to still her. "Shhhh. Listen and answer. We have to do something, but I've got a four-thirty-five flight to catch. I can get back here Monday night. Dinner then?"

"I don't know . . ."

"I do. There's a nice quiet place not far from the hotel. We'll be able to talk. How about it?"

"Mark . . ." She was torn every which way at once.

"Come on, Deanna," he whispered urgently. "We've got something to resolve and we can't do it here." He paused, absorbed both the silence and Deanna's inner turmoil, then went on with even greater conviction. "I'll be in the lobby of the hotel at seven. If you haven't come by seven-fifteen I'll know your answer." Grasping her shoulder, he turned her from him. "Now go! You have a decision to make and I won't be the one to help you."

He was as determined as she was unsure. But his nudge was enough to set her in motion and she continued down the hall without looking back. He was right. It was her decision and hers alone. Somehow, though, she sensed that all the deliberation in the world was academic. She could agonize all weekend and the fact would remain that she wanted to see Mark Birmingham again, plain and simply.

It was barely five past seven when the elevator delivered her to the Hunt International lobby on Monday night. Stepping out, she moved partway to where Mark stood with his back to her, then watched as he felt her presence and turned. Their awareness of each other was uncanny, but she had come to accept it fully. What she couldn't quite accept were the pounding of her pulse and the profusion of second thoughts as to the wisdom of what she was doing. She'd come this far, yet her feet suddenly refused to move.

Mark accommodated her with a spring in his step that she could only understand when he neared. In his pleasure was a fair share of relief. Had he really doubted that she'd come? Certainly he had to know the power he wielded. Yet the touch of uncertainty that gentled his features was as endearing as everything else about the man.

"Hi," he greeted her softly, breaking into a broad white smile that did nothing for her runaway pulse. "I was beginning to worry."

Her own smile was more guarded only in deference to the numerous other pairs of eyes she knew to be watching. "You shouldn't have. It's been only five minutes."

"Five minutes of hell," he growled against her ear, accurately describing her own feelings during those last-minute jitters upstairs. "It wasn't some sort of revenge, was it?"

Deanna grimaced nervously. "If only I'd thought of that. You almost deserve it."

"Almost . . . but not quite. You still came." Putting a hand to her waist, he guided her into the air of a warm September night. "Do you mind walking? We could take a cab if you'd rather."

She sensed she'd be all right once they left the hotel behind. As Mrs. Lawrence Hunt, seeing this handsome man socially, she felt inordinately self-conscious. "The walk will be fine. Nice actually. I don't get to do it very often."

As they started down the street Mark released her and tucked his hands in his pockets. Had Deanna not already known it to be a favorite stance of his she might have been worried; instead she was grateful. Not only did she not want undue attention drawn to them as a couple, but she most definitely didn't need the added stimulation.

It was exciting enough just looking at him. His thick auburn hair waved casually in the light breeze and seemed to have grown longer in the few days since she'd seen him last. Despite his traditional blazer and slacks, shirt and tie, he had the look of the freethinker, the independent, the individualist. Just the opposite of herself . . .

"How was your weekend?" he asked, cutting into her thoughts at a time when she most needed it.

"Very nice."

"Do anything exciting?"

"Exciting?" She laughed. "Not exactly." She didn't usually associate that word with her life. "It was quiet. Pleasant." Not considering, of course, those hours of soul-searching.

"What did you do . . . exactly?"

She felt strangely uncomfortable. "Oh, nothing really. You'd think it very boring." To say the least.

"Try me." He wasn't going to let her off the hook.

Deanna sighed, then yielded. "I had my usual Saturday-morning appointments." She prayed he wouldn't pry. Hairdresser . . . manicurist . . . He'd know how pampered she was. Did she need those weekly dates? "Then I did some shopping. Met some friends for dinner. Yesterday there was a theater benefit for the Heart Association. It was nice."

"But not exciting?" He was obviously quoting her, but she heard no derision in his tone and was grateful.

"Not quite."

"What *would* you consider to be exciting?"

"What would I consider exciting?" She repeated his question, cocking her head to the side in contemplation. A mischievous smile played at the corners of her lips as she shrugged off caution and blurted out her thoughts. "Exciting would be doing something totally impromptu, totally spontaneous. It would be doing something purely for the sake of fun."

"Haven't you ever done that?"

"Me?" She laughed again, this time at her own expense. "You happen to be looking at a model of convention."

"Not always."

"Always!" she rejoined on impulse, then realized her error. "Well . . . almost." The events of the last Tuesday night had defied every convention she'd ever known.

Fortunately Mark wasn't the gloating type and refrained from exploiting her embarrassment. Additionally, their destination loomed immediately ahead.

"Here we are," he said softly, ushering her inside with the faintest touch of his hand to her back.

Those few moments during which they were greeted and seated were precious ones for Deanna. Her composure seemed such a tentative thing when this man was around. Very, very slowly her sheepish blush ebbed.

"Comfortable?" he asked when he'd finally lowered himself into the seat opposite hers.

"Uh-huh. This is lovely. I've never been here before."

"Never? You're kidding. I would have thought you'd made the rounds."

She shook her head. "There's a quaintness here that's delightful. And you're right. It's quiet."

Just right for talking." He paused, watching her closely. "That was interesting—what you said about excitement. Most people would think your life the epitome of excitement. You know—glamour, luxury."

The sadness in Deanna's eyes was unmistakable and sincere. "The grass is always greener," she murmured. "It's too bad. I do like my life and I'm grateful for everything I've got." She frowned as she tried to express her sentiment. "And I feel guilty at not being one-hundred-percent content. But there are times . . . times when I wonder what it would be like to be self-sufficient. You know"—she looked up, almost shy—"to be able to take care of myself. To be independent."

Mark sat back more comfortably. "It has its rewards."

She suddenly saw how neatly he had directed his inquiries. And she was astonished at how easily she had opened up to him. But she was curious as well. It was one of the many reasons behind her decision to come out with him. "Tell me about you, Mark. Do I take it that you're a self-made man?"

"Self-sufficiency isn't limited to the self-made man," he chided her gently. "You could be self-sufficient if you wanted to be." His gaze shifted to the newly arrived waiter and all conversation was momentarily tabled to allow them to order a selection of the northern-Italian offerings in which the small restaurant specialized.

The break in the conversation gave Deanna time to ponder his words. She *couldn't* be self-sufficient, could she? All her life she'd depended on others to provide services for which she was more than willing and able to pay. She simply didn't know *how* to do half the things that other women did as a matter of course. And it bothered her.

"Why so serious?" Mark asked, leaning forward and taking her hand. Quite unknowingly she curled her fingers tightly around his, needing the reassurance of their warmth.

"I don't know. I guess we all brood now and then."

Misinterpreting the cause of her anxiety, he took a different tack, one that was no less contemplative. "You're not upset at being with me, are you?"

"Oh, no! I wanted to come. I may be a fool for having done it, but I *did* want to come."

"And the other night—have you resolved that in your mind?"

She had no doubt to which night he referred. When she tried to extricate her hand he tightened his around it. "No," she admitted in a more subdued voice. "I'm still having trouble there."

"Cart before the horse, eh?" He grinned and her heart flipflopped dangerously. Yet she couldn't resist a smile.

"Since we seem to be into clichés, yes. You could say

that. We're doing it backwards, aren't we?" she asked softly.

"It depends how you want to see it. There are many different kinds of relationships. There's the physical. There's the emotional. There's the superficial . . . and the profound. Look at it this way. What we did was spontaneous, not to mention physically profound. If that wasn't exciting enough for you, I give up."

"Now you're making fun of me," she teased him back, unable to sustain discomfort in the face of his good humor. If only he were more resistible, she mused, appreciating afresh the blatant quality of his masculinity. Even the dim lighting in the restaurant couldn't hide his eyes' spirited gleam.

"No, just making a point. But I won't dwell on it." He slanted her a look of suspicion. "You probably did that all weekend anyway . . . between those, uh, pleasant events you found so unexciting."

"You're perceptive." To say the least. "But what about you? How was your weekend?"

"Busy. A lot of running around. And I did a lot of work. Drafting type of thing."

"You often spend the weekend working?"

"When I'm doing something I enjoy as much as last weekend's work."

Had Deanna's mind not been stalled in one particular vein, she might have questioned him about that work. Instead she smiled almost timidly. "No . . . wild date?"

His gaze leveled. "No. I had all I could handle thinking about tonight."

"And . . . if I hadn't shown up?"

"I'd have been crushed."

"You're either very honest or . . . slightly off balance," she joked; either way she felt disturbed herself. Reluctant to open that discussion again, she shot him a scolding glance and veered off in a different direction. "I meant

what I said about the hospital plans. They're wonderful."
He dipped his head in silent thanks and said nothing.
Deanna had the strange sensation that there was a
method behind his silence. "Will you tell me more about
your work?" she prodded quietly, mindful of his earlier
evasion.

Mark's smile was crooked, knowing. "You're not afraid
of learning about me now?"

She hesitated, then feigned a scowl in admission of
defeat. "It looks like I'm stuck with you, seeing as you've
been chosen to design the hospital. Call it a business
interest."

His eyes said he didn't believe her for a minute, yet his
words were almost accommodating. Almost. "I have to
admit that I was surprised that you knew nothing of my
involvement before last Thursday. Does Warner make
every decision himself?"

"He has a board of directors."

"And you? What's your role in it all?"

"I suppose I'm the most powerful . . . and the least. If I
want to disagree with any decision, I have veto power.
I'm the head of the foundation—nominally, at least. More
practically speaking, Bob is in a better position to be able
to make decisions. My knowledge of business is limited
and I'm not even sure that I want to be that involved with
the everyday workings of the whole thing. Bob assumes
that I'll see things his way."

"And do you?"

"I've had no reason for doubt so far. He was wonderful when—" She faltered, hesitant to go on until the man
across from her coaxed her silently. "Bob was wonderful
when my husband died. He took over at a time when I
didn't know what was happening. It's an overwhelming
thought—being suddenly left at the helm of a multi-
million-dollar setup."

"You'd never had any part in it before?" Mark asked.

Deanna tried to shrug away her mild embarrassment. "In Larry's mind women were to be pampered. He took pride in giving me things, in sheltering me from every worry in the world. It was almost as if his success was defined by the quality of my . . . my . . . protection."

The wine steward arrived and proceeded to present, uncork and pour their wine, so she fell silent. It occurred to her that she'd never opened up to a person as she'd just done. Until this airing, her thoughts on the subject of Larry and her role in his life had been solely in her own mind, never shared. It was a frightening experience to hear them spill forth so freely.

When they were alone once more she remained quiet, eyes and hands on her wineglass, brows gathered in the beginnings of a frown. But Mark was not about to let her brood. Lifting his glass he proposed a gentle toast.

"To the memory of the husband who very obviously adored you. And to you—the warm and giving woman he nurtured. May nothing stop your emergence from your cocoon into the exquisite butterfly I know you to be."

When he'd begun Deanna had lifted her glass quite innocently. As she'd heard the words, however, her hand had started to shake. Fearful of her unsteadiness, she put the glass down and lowered her suddenly tear-filled eyes. She was unaware that Mark had moved until he sat much closer, having deftly relocated his chair to the side of the table.

"I'm sorry, Deanna," he whispered, lifting his hand to her face as though to shield her emotion from the world. She felt his fingers inching from her cheek toward her ear and then into the thickness of the hair beyond her temple. On pure instinct she turned her face toward him. His lips were inches away. "I'm sorry, honey. I didn't mean to upset you. Damn it, I seem to have a knack for doing that!"

Hearing his self-reproach, she forced a whispered "I'm all right." But a single tear escaped her closed lids, and seeking shelter, she leaned forward to put her temple against his cheek. His own protective impulse had been stirred and she savored the comfort he offered as his hand slid down to lightly caress her neck.

"I'm sorry," he whispered again.

But she felt the tenseness of his jaw and drew back to look at him. "It's all right. What you said was . . . lovely. But scary. I feel . . . confused."

Her confusion had never been greater than at that moment, when his features were so close and, in their way, so very dear. Even the lingering moisture in her eyes couldn't distort the vulnerability she saw again on his face. It was mixed with worry and a strange hint of fear and she only knew that she wanted to ease it.

Without stopping to consider what she was doing, she leaned forward and kissed him gently, offering her own form of solace. He was warm and fresh smelling beneath her touch and when he responded she found satisfaction. It was only the ghost of a bearded roughness on his cheek that alerted her to the fact that her lips had quite happily begun to wander.

She drew back abruptly, fearful of what she might find. But the look she saw in Mark's eyes held no ridicule. Rather she saw a smoldering desire that took her back in time to another night, his hotel room, his bed. Her entire body felt the heat of his gaze and she trembled with a longing she simply couldn't deny.

Fortunately Mark seemed to come to his senses. Clearing his throat, he shook his head as though to free himself of a daze and reached for his wineglass once more. "To whatever the future holds," he whispered hoarsely, took a sip, then offered his own glass to her. Deanna put her lips where his had been seconds before and sealed the toast. Then, as though on cue, their dinner arrived.

The air between them never quite cooled, though. For one thing, Mark stayed where he was by Deanna's side, leaning back in his seat while the waiter relaid his setting, holding her hand beneath the table all the while. For another, the smoldering light never totally left his eyes— nor hers, for that matter. Her senses seemed fine-tuned to everything about him, reacting to the shape of his hand, the pulse in his throat, the rakish fall of hair across his forehead. And his thigh rubbing against hers on occasion drove her to distraction. She remembered all too well its bare form, leanly muscled, hair-roughened, tanned and strong, and the memory heated her blood.

He took pity on her, however, and opened up about his work, though one small sly part of her suspected he did it in defense against his own desires as much as for her information. She sensed that he would have been content to sit and stare at her, hold her hand, touch her leg—do whatever else was possible within the confines of the small restaurant. But they were relatively hamstrung —he reluctantly, she gratefully. Again she feared the force of her feelings and the future to which he had so poignantly toasted.

"I suppose you could say I'm a self-made man," he began with a modest shrug. "I built the firm from scratch. It's taken over twelve years, but we're proud of the name we've established."

"From the look of those hospital plans you've got every right to be proud. But tell me—why Savannah?"

His smile was innocent. "I like it. It's a beautiful city. This entire area—the South—appealed to me. When I was first setting up shop there seemed to be a lot of opportunities here for an aspiring architect. That's proven to be the case."

"You had no ties elsewhere?"

"Family? No. I grew up in Delaware, but my parents are gone. My only brother is a professor at UCLA."

"You have a brother?" she asked, excited. "Older or younger?"

"Older by nine years. My parents married late in life, had my brother, then I came along even later. It was hard on them. We weren't the quietest of kids."

"Few are."

"Were you?"

"Quiet?" She grinned. "Oh, yes. The perfect lady."

"Even as a child?"

"Even then," she quipped, but the grin died suddenly. As always Mark drove to the crux of the issue. "Why, Deanna? Why such a docile child? No rebellion? No spoiled-brat syndrome? It's unusual."

She took a deep breath and thought back on those childhood days. "I learned a sad lesson early in life," she whispered. Mark held her gaze. When she would have ended there his silent demand brought out the story. "I had a brother too." The softness of her voice held years of pain. "He was ten years my senior. I idolized him. Of course, he pampered me much as everyone else did." A trace of self-derision tinged her words in passing but vanished quickly. "Patrick was the rebel in the family, though. It got worse as he got older." She frowned. "I still can't understand why he had to make a point of defying everyone and everything."

"What happened?" Mark's low voice cut into her brooding. She looked up sharply, needing an instant to readjust.

"He was killed in a boating accident. Carelessness. Bad weather. He'd taken it upon himself to sail a thirty-three-foot ketch from Maine to Virginia. Don't ask me why—lord knows he didn't need the money. I guess it was a lark. He was twenty at the time and an experienced sailor. But the girl he brought along—his only crew—had no experience. The boat was ill equipped and Pat wasn't particularly interested in life jackets at all. He'd defy anything. Unfortunately he didn't have a chance when they hit the shoals. He lost his balance and banged his head. The Coast Guard assumed he was unconscious before he hit the sea. His girl had no idea what to do to help him. It was foggy and rough . . ."

Mark took her hand and tucked it between his own, stroking her fingers while the silence worked as a buffer between past and present. "Life is so fragile," he whispered, lost in his own thoughts for a minute.

"So you vowed that you wouldn't follow in his footsteps?"

"It wasn't his footsteps that frightened me as much as the pain in those he left behind. My parents were devastated. I was ten at the time, old enough to understand and share their agony. I guess I decided that nothing was worth that. So"—she inhaled slowly—"I behaved myself."

Needing a bit of humor, Mark grinned. "Is that the past tense I hear?"

"Is that wishful thinking I hear?" she shot right back, clutching at humor as a way of distancing the past. It was so comfortable being with Mark, talking with him. Again she'd told him things she'd never told another. And yet again she felt herself nearing shaky ground. A change of subject seemed the safest course. "Does your work take you traveling often?"

His gaze narrowed. "Sneaky . . ."

"Does it?" She could also be persistent. "Bob mentioned the work you've done in West Virginia."

"West Virginia, Oklahoma, Missouri, Iowa, Michigan . . . it's spread out more than I'd expected when I chose

Savannah as my home. It sometimes seems that I'm never there."

"Does it bother you to travel?"

"Sometimes. Hotel rooms can be pretty cold—yours excepted, naturally."

"Naturally." She grinned, then sobered. "But I'd think the excitement of your work would overshadow the drawbacks of traveling."

Mark chuckled. "Excitement. That word again. Yes, it's exciting. The traveling does get lonely though." His gaze grew pointed. "It would be nice to have someone with me every so often. For that matter, if there were someone waiting at home I'd cut down on the traveling at this stage."

"Why isn't there?" she blurted out spontaneously.

"Someone waiting?" He arched a brow and she ached to trace its commanding line with her finger. Instead she made a fist and nodded silently. Mark sighed. "It's been a long haul up the ladder, Deanna. We self-made men don't get much help at the start. It's a cutthroat world out there. To get the best jobs one not only has to be a skilled architect but an endless worker. It doesn't leave much time for relationships." Suddenly he seemed to be the one whose need to express himself superseded the need for reserve and he elaborated readily. "I've known women over the years. I haven't stayed alone, lonely, for want of companionship. But you can be *with* a woman . . . and then you can *be* with a woman. The first is detached, the second involved. For the first time in my life, now I want the latter."

Fresh coffee was set before them and Deanna sipped slowly. "What *do* you want, Mark? How do you envision your future?" She asked him outwardly as a friend, all the while trying to ignore the inner naggings that went far beyond simple friendship.

Mark's abrupt intensity was a direct assault on her emotions. His eyes—deep, rich chocolate, a shade darker than her own—spoke with that same quiet need she'd heard before. "My future? Ideally?" He leaned closer and spoke more softly, but no less urgently. "With my profession established now, I want to build a home."

"Surely you've got one in Savannah—"

"No, Deanna. I'm not talking about the physical fact of a place to live. You're right. I've got that—a house in Savannah, land in the mountains north of here. But I don't have a *home* that a woman makes, a home to come to, one to stay in. Perhaps I'm old-fashioned, but I want a woman there to greet me. I want a family. Children. I'm not getting any younger and there is that . . . void. Professional success has its limits."

A wife. Family. *Children.* The pain that ripped through her was as harsh as any Deanna had ever had to bear. Once more she was engulfed by a swell of inadequacy. Mark needed all the things she couldn't give him. It was all so unfair. Despite the force of their physical attraction for one another and the further compatibility this evening had evidenced, Deanna knew she was out of the running. He wanted a wife totally devoted to him, yet she couldn't even cook a meal. And he wanted children. Nine years of marriage to Larry and she'd never conceived. Larry hadn't pushed the issue, had discouraged her from having tests on the grounds that being a father didn't matter to him. As a result of his vehemence she had steadfastly denied the fact that being a mother *did* matter to *her*. But then Larry had died and it had become a moot point. All the mourning in the world couldn't provide her with a child to love after the fact. Larry had loved her, limitations and all. She couldn't possibly ask Mark to do the same. Not when those things meant so much to him . . .

"Deanna? Deanna! What's wrong?"

His concerned tone snapped her from the nightmare. But she'd withdrawn into her shell and could only shake her head. He stared at her face, devoid now of color, paid the bill quickly with cash and then, with a muffled oath, he took her hand.

"Come on. Let's get out of here."

# 6

~~~~~~~~~~~~~~~~~~~

The fresh air was what she needed. Mark's protective arm about her shoulder was not. She found herself nestling far too snugly against him, selfishly absorbing his comfort, all the while feeling guilty about how little she could offer in return.

She let her arm curve beneath his jacket and around his lean waist. They walked slowly, silently and in perfect step. Occasionally their eyes met. It was at one of those times that Deanna realized she was well on her way to falling in love with Mark, if she hadn't done so already. He was so special, had been from the first. She should have been able to see it coming—not that there was anything she could have done to stop it. It was beautiful and inevitable and terribly, terribly hopeless.

"Okay now?" he murmured into the soft auburn sheen of her hair.

"Uh-huh," she lied, wanting to pretend that her hopelessness didn't exist.

"Want to talk about it?"

She shook her head. "No. Not tonight. It's too lovely."

A tremor passed the length of Mark's body and she wondered for a minute if it was her own. When his arm tightened reflexively around her, she sighed her pleasure. If only she could retreat into fantasy again. If only she could disregard every reality but Mark, his magnificent body and her burgeoning desire for him.

Reading her thoughts, Mark hurried her around a corner into a small alleyway and took her into his arms before she could begin to question the wisdom of the move. His lips came down on hers with the force of his own pent-up need, igniting a response that had been similarly building in her all evening. Nothing could dampen the hunger exploding between them as their arms wound convulsively around one another and their lips consumed each other greedily.

"Deanna . . . Deanna . . . I need you so much. . . ." he rasped, dragging his mouth from hers to devour the faintly scented skin of her neck. His hands seemed everywhere, trailing white-hot fire along her arms and around her waist, covering her ribs and rising to her breasts as she strained in torment against him.

She heard his love words only in a daze, for she was engrossed in the touching as well. This was a momentary bonanza—this dark, dark alleyway. For these few reckless moments she was free again. Her fingers pressed through the fabric of his suit to adore the vibrant sinews that stretched virilely beneath. She reached to his shoulders and arched catlike against him, then let her hands fall the length of his arms to his hips and thighs. As his kiss deepened into scorching tongue play, she stroked the steel of those thighs, moving slowly inward until he sucked in a breath of frustration.

"Oh, honey . . . I could take you here and now. . . ."

"I know," she whispered, wanting it as well. "I know,

106

Mark. . . ." Her body ached with the hollowness he'd created, the hollowness only he could fill. This time it was her mouth that sought an urgent kiss, her lips that underscored the internal cry.

Then, slowly, a foreign sound penetrated the stillness of the dark alley. It was the steady beat of slow applause, one deliberate clap after the other, until both Deanna and Mark stared toward it in shock. Mark's arms tightened protectively, pulling her slightly behind him. But there was no cause for fear. The drunk in the alley couldn't even stand. As it was his speech was slurred, nearly incomprehensible.

"Verrrra . . . goooood . . . shoow . . ." The applause continued in its monotonous rhythm.

"Damn!" Mark seethed, hurrying Deanna from the alley to the sidewalk once more and heading at a faster clip toward the hotel. She wasn't sure whether he was angry, embarrassed or frustrated. She herself felt all three, plus a fourth emotion: remorse. But there was little time for thought, or to regain her composure, before the Hunt International came into sight. Only then did Mark's pace slacken and his arm fall from her shoulder to his side.

He said nothing and she matched his silence. They might have been two strangers who just happened to arrive at the hotel simultaneously, each with his head down, each deep in thought. It was still early, barely ten. The lobby was busy for a Monday evening, the elevator nearly filled.

This time Mark's room was on the twenty-ninth floor. When the elevator stopped there and he firmly seized her hand, Deanna was taken by surprise. She hadn't expected a repeat of this when she'd decided to have dinner with him. Or had she?

With a still half-full elevator behind her and Mark standing commandingly before her she had little choice but to follow him. As soon as she heard the elevator door close, though, she forced out her protest.

"I don't want to come with you," she whispered hoarsely. The pain of duplicity was sheer agony. She wanted more than anything to be with him. It was foresight that condemned the act. "Mark . . . please!"

He paid her no heed. He released her hand only when he'd reached his door, quickly inserted the card to unlock it, then almost gruffly led her inside. Once there he shut the door and bolted it. It seemed that he had only one purpose in mind. Deanna read it in the lambency of his gaze as he struggled to control his emotions.

"You said we'd talk," she reminded him in a fearful whisper, though the demon now was herself. Nothing would have pleased her more than to have thrown herself into his arms in an utterly selfish drive toward satisfaction. Was this all she had to give him—her body for his gratification? Even there she was no expert.

Mark swallowed hard and spoke thickly, his hands cocked tensely on his hips. "How in the hell can we talk when I can't think straight? The only truth seems to be our lovemaking. Primal communication. No pretense. No fear. Commitment . . . even if it's fleeting." Pausing, he studied her rounded eyes and gentled. "You look so pretty, Deanna. Your dress, your hair . . . but all I can think of is stripping you naked, taking that clip from your hair, making love to you until *you* can't think straight!"

Deanna caught her breath. Unable to argue with anything he'd said, she took a step back and shook her head at the urging of reason, but already her limbs were weakening. Already her pulse had sped up in anticipation. If this were the only gift she had to offer Mark, perhaps she might even be able to make it special. She'd need his help, though. Already she felt the fear of inadequacy.

Stepping forward she crossed the small distance between them. Her hands lifted to his waist and she watched them slide up over the smooth fabric of his shirt until they rested on the corded swells of his chest. His heart raced beneath her fingertips, the first note of encouragement. Only then did she look up at him.

"I'm afraid, Mark . . . of so much. I can't ask you to understand what I don't understand myself. But I do want to please you." Her voice lowered to a barely audible plea. "Will you . . . help me?"

She couldn't quite fathom the incredulous look on his face. It was as though she'd spoken a foreign language. But then he answered and her own face adopted the same look.

"Me . . . help you? Deanna, you don't need any help. You please me just as you are now, just as you were last time we were together. It's those memories that are driving me insane! I need you again. *You!*"

A silent message coursed between them. At that instant there were only the two of them. All else in the world was irrelevant. Yielding to the longing that threatened to smother her from within, Deanna cried out as she wrapped her arms around his neck and pulled herself close against him. "I need you, Mark. I need you to love me," she murmured dazedly, unaware of her words, mindful only of her frustration at every thin barrier between them.

The frustration was mutual. Mark kissed her once, sweeping the honeyed sweetness from the far recesses of her mouth with a thrust that shook her, then set her back. They undressed wordlessly, never taking their eyes from each other. When Deanna wore nothing but her silken bra and panties, she stopped. Having just stepped from his trousers Mark straightened slowly. At the sight of his briefs she burst into a light-hearted grin.

"Now what's so funny?" he growled, sweeping her off her feet and into his arms as he headed for the bedroom.

"Blue-and-white stripes?" she laughed breathlessly. "I love it!"

He lowered her gently to the bed. Seconds later he was upon her. "Pretty smart, aren't you?" he drawled down at her, sliding his body intimately over hers. "You forgot your hair. Here, let me do it."

He sat up beside her, reached down and with deliberate slowness unclipped the gold clasp that had secured the thick fall. His touch held a wealth of tenderness as he finger-combed her hair around her head on the pillow.

Meanwhile she reveled in the bareness of his chest. Broad, tanned and warm, its virile expanse beckoned. Reaching out, she touched him, then sat up with a bolt and nudged him down until he was the one on his back. If this was her gift, she'd make it good.

Crouching over him, she lowered her mouth to his, moving her lips with sensual delight, teasing him, tasting him until he held her head still so he could plumb the depth she'd knowingly denied. At the instant she began to lose herself in him, she pulled away. She had to be controlled, to know what she was doing, if she hoped to pleasure him to the fullest.

Her hands paved the way, then her lips followed over a trail that began at his mouth and wound down his throat to the firmness of his chest. His skin tasted tart. The flatness of his nipples soon grew hard beneath the pads of her thumbs. Her hair whispered over his skin, falling around her face, a delicate veil of passion.

Mark groaned, squirmed, lifted her under her arms until she was over him, then kissed her fiercely. "You're a minx!" he moaned into her mouth. But his tongue was gentle, tasting her mouth until Deanna was the one to cry out.

Suddenly she found herself on her back, looking up as Mark unhooked the front closure of her bra and eased the material from her creamy-soft fullness. She watched, mesmerized, as his head lowered, his mouth surrounded the rosy shadow of her breast, his teeth closed carefully around her nipple's peak. Then she let her lids drop and concentrated on sensation as he played with that nub, rolling it with his tongue, tugging until the pull bridged the far distance to her loins and she whimpered his name.

At that point she barely recalled her intention. What little she did know she was unable to enact. He'd commandeered her senses as if bent on retribution for the week of cold showers he'd had to endure and she simply didn't have the strength to deny herself any of this electrifying glory. If she lacked something as a seductress it was no longer important. Mark's body strained as urgently as did hers.

He sat up only to hook his thumbs beneath the lace of her panties and ease them over her hips. Then he rolled to his side to shimmy from the blue-and-white striped briefs she'd kidded him about. But she didn't kid him now as he returned to kneel by her side in momentary awe of her body. Nor did she kid him on his obvious state of arousal.

Instead she rose to meet him, kneeling before him suddenly with the desperate urge to declare her love. That was the ultimate vulnerability, though. The time wasn't right.

Her eyes spoke softly as she inched toward him and her hands grew emboldened by the love swelling within her. In as natural a move as she'd ever made, she reached to touch him. One hand slid over the flesh of his hips to his firm flank, the other to the proof of his need.

He gasped her name and drew her closer as she stroked him. She found her own blood heating as she continued to warm his. Indeed, her ministrations affected her nearly as much as they did him, and she brought her mouth to meet his with a near violence she would never have believed had she been functioning rationally. But she wasn't. She'd become a creature of love, motivated by it, driven by it, inspired by it until it was the only reality that existed.

Dizzy from the force of passion's eddy, they tumbled to the bed. Then, in a moment of choreographic precision, their bodies came together at last. Deanna was as moist and ready as Mark was firm to fill her. The night was broken by their cries as they seemed to shift and eclipse one another, climbing ever higher until first Deanna, then Mark, reached, sustained, shattered, then slowly descended from the far-flung ecstasy of fulfillment.

Long afterward they lay in each other's arms, their bodies damp and spent. Deanna listened as Mark's breathing grew gradually more even and he dozed off, exhausted. She snuggled closer, her head pillowed on his shoulder, her cheek against his chest, her hand falling to lie on his stomach.

The slow cadence of his breathing should have been a sedative for her, but her eyes were wide open, sleep the furthest thing from mind. Unashamed for once, she studied his body. His stomach was flat, his hips lean. He lay still, drained of passion. He'd brought her such pleasure.

She tipped her head back to study his face, at rest, yet no less manly. What she felt went far beyond physical arousal. Without doubt, she loved this man deeply. Emotion surged through her, filling her as fully as he had filled her earlier. She loved Mark . . . and she had no idea what she was going to do!

He opened a heavy-lidded eye with slow reluctance. Deanna reached up and kissed his cheek. "I've got to go," she murmured softly. "You go back to sleep."

"Stay, Deanna," he whispered, closing his eyes again. "I can't."

"We have . . . to talk. . . ."

"Another time." Very gently, she untangled herself

from him and quietly dressed. By the time she was ready to leave he was sleeping soundly. Indulging herself for a final moment, she stood looking down at him. He was sprawled on his back, his head fallen sideways on the pillow. His hair was in disarray from their wild passion; his skin had a lingering sheen. He was long and strong, breathtaking in repose. But his body blurred before her when her eyes filled with tears. If only she could stay. He wanted so much, though, *needed* so much. If only she could have been the one. Blotting her eyes with the back of her hand, she turned and left.

It took every bit of her self-command to rouse herself from bed the next morning. She couldn't have slept for more than two or three hours and had a wicked headache as proof. Given her choice, she would have liked to burrow into oblivion for the day. But there were things to be done, people expecting her. And she felt an urgent need to be away from the suite when Mark called—as she was sure he would.

All the agony of the lonely hours of the night had been futile. She hadn't resolved a thing; the endless battle continued. Was this what she'd invited when she'd surrendered to fantasy one short week earlier? Could she have known she'd fall in love for real?

She breakfasted earlier and more quickly than usual, calling on deep reserves to present her usual image of composure to the world as she prayed that Mark wouldn't show. That particular prayer was answered. As for the escape she'd hoped to achieve by dashing off to the hospital, it evaded her. Throughout the morning, despite every diversion, her thoughts were her own and she brooded darkly. Mark deserved so much more than she could give him. She was a product of twenty-nine years of careful molding and she doubted she could ever break free.

**113**

Back at her suite she barely picked at the cold sweet-and-sour salmon Irma had poached for her lunch.

"Is everything all right, Mrs. Hunt?"

"Yes." She dragged herself from dark reflections. "Uh, yes. I guess I'm just not hungry, Irma. I'm sorry."

"You're feeling all right?"

"I'm fine."

The housekeeper knew her place and didn't question her further. But she was watchful, much as she had been the night before when Deanna had returned to the suite so late with a flush of rose on her cheeks and her hair tumbling wildly about her shoulders. Then there were those phone calls this morning so soon after Deanna had left, and again before she'd returned. When Irma had mentioned them, Deanna had shrugged with an indifference she might have carried off had it not been for the betraying tremor of her lower lip. Something was happening, Irma knew. Whether it was good or bad remained to be seen.

In her room Deanna rehearsed every excuse in the book before reaching the conclusion that she simply couldn't avoid the office. If it wasn't that afternoon it would be the next day or Thursday, and she doubted she'd have anything more to say then than she had now. With a deep sigh of resignation she had Henry bring the car around.

An hour later she was in the office, trying to pretend she was the same woman who'd spent every other Tuesday and Thursday there for what suddenly seemed forever. But she'd changed. The keen gaze she shot warily toward the door every now and then gave evidence of that. Fortunately, she wasn't with any one person long enough to betray her unease.

The hours dragged. She was busy enough, yet the slim gold watch on her wrist seemed to operate in slow motion. With each glance at the door she expected to see *his* face. Yet . . . nothing. Two. Two-thirty. Three. Three-thirty. Nothing. At four o'clock she gave up all pretense of collectedness. Wrapping her work up quickly, she spoke briefly with Bob, then left as furtively as possible.

To her list of self-directed epithets she now added another: coward. Not only had she not had the courage to question Bob Warner about Mark's whereabouts, she'd taken to avoiding Mark after all. As she let herself into the suite she felt ashamed. What had happened to the poised, dignified woman Larry Hunt had left behind? This new woman might have known the richness of love, but Deanna wasn't sure she liked the side effects.

She had barely started dinner when the doorbell rang. There was no question in her mind as to who it was. Nor had she any doubt that, for the sake of her self-respect alone, she had to see him.

Laying her fork quietly on the plate, she waited. The voices from the foyer were muted; then Mark appeared at the archway to the breakfast room in which she sat. Irma was immediately behind him, clenching her hands. Deanna took the situation in at a glance.

"It's all right, Irma. Mr. Birmingham is welcome." Irma relaxed visibly, smiled more shyly and left. Mark, on the other hand, grew more tense. He didn't move from the door, simply stared at her.

"Have a seat, Mark." She gestured, the near-perfect hostess. She would have stood had it not been for the familiar weakness in her knees. It wasn't fair that she could be so affected by any man.

"Deanna?"

She averted her eyes in sheer defense. "Please sit. Have you eaten?"

"You know I haven't."

Looking out toward the kitchen, she raised her voice.

"Irma?" A soft rustle of skirts brought the woman back. "If you could set another place, Mr. Birmingham will join me for dinner."

She heard Mark add a gentle "If it's no trouble," heard the smile in his words and finally looked up to see the broad grin with which he had melted Irma's hesitancy in an instant.

"Oh, it's no trouble at all, Mr. Birmingham. I won't be but a minute." She whisked away again, leaving them momentarily alone.

Deanna's eyes dropped to her lap, where her napkin was bunched in her fist. She was marginally aware that Mark had settled into a chair opposite her.

"You've been avoiding me," he stated calmly, his tension in check.

She met his gaze with a shot of petulance. "I could say the same about you." The best defense was a good offense, so they said. But this had come too easily. Shocked, she realized that one part of her had been hurt when he hadn't appeared at the office.

"I called here several times this morning. You weren't in. Then, when I returned to your office late this afternoon, you'd already left."

"You did stop at the office?" she asked more contritely.

"Of course! I was out at the site. Didn't Warner tell you that?"

"No."

"And you didn't ask." It was a statement. He understood her too well.

"No."

"I see," he murmured, propping his elbows on the arms of the chair, interlacing his fingers, then resting them against the firm line of his mouth. He seemed to deliberate as he sat staring at her and only blinked away his concentration when Irma returned bearing a tray and his meal.

Deanna had waited until he had food before him to pick up her fork once more. Now, as she stared down at the *boeuf bourguignone,* she felt no appetite whatsoever. Her stomach had begun to churn, a victim of the whirling emotions that made clear thought an effort. Mark, on the contrary, seemed to have suddenly revived.

"This is delicious. Does she cook like this all the time?"

Deanna's head shot up. "Irma? Yes, she's a jewel." When Mark continued to eat, Deanna could only settle back in her chair and watch him in amazement. What had become of his anger or tension or whatever it was that had possessed him when he'd arrived? He ate slowly, thoughtfully. Perhaps he too was working it all out in his mind. Perhaps he'd have better success than she was having.

As the minutes passed, Deanna found herself growing amused. The man had really been hungry. Her smile came easily when she finally broke the silence. "Are you always a grump on an empty stomach?"

Satisfied with something, at least, he sat back in a lazy pose. "For the answer to that, Deanna, you'll just have to stick around. I wasn't thrilled to wake up to a cold bed this morning."

"You were dead to the world! I told you I was leaving."

"That didn't make the fact any easier to take." He had grown more serious, his eyes as intense as they had ever been. "Why did you leave? You could have spent the night."

"I couldn't have—"

"You could have . . . if you'd wanted to. Irma would have kept your secret if you'd called to tell her you'd be back in the morning. She doesn't look like such an ogre. And she would have been flattered by your trust."

Deanna frowned, reflecting on his smooth and ready answers. One part of her ached to blurt out her deepest thoughts, those dreadful fears. Might he have solutions for those? But the more immediate worry was Mark's strange look as he stared at her.

"Is something wrong?" she asked more timidly than she would have liked.

"I was just about to ask you the same thing. What's wrong, Deanna? What's going on in that mind of yours that you can be so wary of me after last night?"

"Last night . . ." She breathed the words as though they were part dream, part nightmare.

But Mark pounced on her words, leaning suddenly forward. "Last night you loved me, Deanna. You can deny it as much as you want, but a woman doesn't respond to a man that way unless she feels it here." He thumped his chest. She couldn't deny the truth of that, but it didn't change the facts.

"It was one night, Mark—"

"It was *two* nights . . . two nights in bed, plus all those others just thinking about each other. We have something good. Why can't you face that?"

Closing her eyes for a moment of respite, she shook her head. "We've been through all this," she whispered. When she looked up again her eyes held a sober poignancy. "I'm not good for you, Mark. Last night . . . today . . . there's your proof. I have other obligations. I'm not free."

The abruptness with which he shot from his seat to lean on the table startled her. "That's a lot of garbage!"

But he'd stirred her own anger and she lashed back at being pushed so hard. "I take back what I said about your being a grump on an empty stomach. You just must have gotten up on the wrong side of bed!"

"Damn right I did!" he exclaimed, his eyes flashing darkly. "I crawled all over your side looking for you before I fell on the floor!"

Unable to resist the image, Deanna brust into a smug

laugh. "Serves you right for falling asleep on me like that!"

In a split-second turnabout, Mark grew sheepish. His chin fell to his chest and he scratched the back of his head. "Boy, was I exhausted. Must have been all those restless nights in between." When he shook his head again, Deanna felt her anger begin to dissolve, only to have it rise again moments later under his renewed assault. "So we're back on the ground floor, hmmm?" There was no humor in his straight gaze. "Back to the yes-no's, you can–I can't's, you could–I couldn't t's."

What could she say to that? He'd been right about one thing, she mused. She *had* loved him the night before— mind, body and soul. As for the rest, it couldn't work. His fantasy was misdirected. He wanted a woman, an active, capable woman. And he wanted children. She'd only frustrate him on both counts.

"You know, Deanna," he began, moving around the table until he towered over her. "I know that something frightens you, but I can't figure out exactly what it is. We work on the same wavelength on almost everything else. On this, though, you're shutting me out. It's like there's a block and I can't seem to break through." As he paused the muscle at his jaw flexed, a product of his taut-held control, a control that seemed ready to snap.

"What is it with you?" he spat out vehemently. "Have you got something against happiness? Some kind of martyr complex?" Even the chill in his voice didn't prepare her for his follow-up. "Your brother dies, therefore you become the model daughter. Your husband dies, so you've become the model widow. Damn it— wake up! Life doesn't work that way. No one's asking you to pay for their deaths!"

For an instant Deanna sat stunned. "You're wrong, Mark," she whispered, needing desperately to deny his charge. "That's not it at all." But she was frightened, unable to go on. And Mark knew that.

Again he lowered his head, this time rubbing the back of his neck in the process. "Well, Deanna, I can't pull it out of you, *whatever* it is. Maybe you do need time. . . ."

Turning on his heel, he left her alone. She heard his voice in the hall, saying something to Irma; then the front door shut with definite finality. She'd never felt so alone in her life.

# 7

He had said that she needed time and that was precisely what he gave her. Though he sat across the dining room from her the next morning, he was a virtual stranger. If he had accused her of placing a block between them, things were now reversed. He looked at her; she looked at him. Whether he read the message of sadness she sent, she would never know, because his eyes were an impenetrable mahogany shade on his soul and she was totally shut out.

That was the last she saw of him for over a week. When she went to breakfast Thursday he wasn't there. Nor was he at the Hunt offices that afternoon. This time, though, she did mention him to Bob.

"I love the preliminary plans for the hospital." She put on her finest smile. "Mark's done a great job."

"He's a talented man." An understatement, she reflected ruefully.

"Uh-huh." She paused, feigning sudden puzzlement.

121

"I haven't seen him around. Is he all done here for a while?"

Bob sensed nothing amiss. "No, no. He'll be back. There was some sort of emergency that took him back to Savannah yesterday. He'll be in touch."

Deanna wondered. The weekend was a particularly quiet one for her and she spent hour upon hour wondering. The first of the week came and went; still she wondered. Tuesday, Wednesday and Thursday passed with no sign of him at either the hotel or the office. The subtle inquiries she made gleaned nothing. By Friday she was tired of wondering.

Time. An entire week. What insights had she gained? She'd begun to analyze the true nature of her fear and now saw that it extended far beyond the cooking of a single meal, even beyond her inability to conceive a child. Her fear was of the new and the different, both of which Mark Birmingham represented. In the brief times they'd spent together he'd demanded and drawn more from her than any other person had ever done. And she knew he would continue to do so if she agreed to pursue the relationship. In her near-thirty years she'd always known what to expect from life and those around her. Mark was from a different world, one that was strange to her. He was an unknown in so many regards. That frightened her.

The days of soul-searching had also drawn her thoughts to the fantasy, that original fantasy that had fused her to Mark in the first place. She recalled the fleeting fears she'd had at the time that the real man might not meet her overblown expectations. Now she understood that fear was a double-edged sword and she was convinced that *she* was the one who wouldn't measure up. Mark was bound to be disappointed as time went on.

She was neither an intellectual nor an aggressor and

she'd never functioned independently in her life. What could she offer Mark beyond poise and social standing? Despite all the money she had, she felt helpless. It was much as it had been for those ecstatic nights in his arms. Naked, she could only offer him her love.

Her love. That was the crux, the only thing of which she was increasingly sure as the days melded one into the next. She had only to think of him and her heart ached with a need beyond the physical, though, heaven help her, that was there too in the emptiness she felt. It was worst at night—the physical torment. Recollections of the feel of his skin, the soft-textured hair on his arms and legs ruffling beneath her fingertips, the contrasting butter-smoothness of his hips gliding under her palms. Images of his strength encircling her, enhancing her. Memories of his passion, wild and demanding, offering her a unique brand of fulfillment at the cost of her love.

Her love. Wanting to be with him . . . yet afraid. Needing to give to him . . . yet afraid. Craving a tomorrow beside him . . . yet afraid. In the end it all boiled down to one question: did she love him enough to fight that fear?

Friday morning broke with a heavy mist, a dull, dark day to match her mood. Galvanized solely by habit she breakfasted in the dining room, then returned to the suite. She was driven to the club, played tennis, then returned home. She even had Henry drop her at her favorite boutique in search of a new fall dress that might brighten up her spirits, but she returned to the hotel as empty-handed as she was empty-hearted.

Unable to face her own lonely company for another minute, she changed into jeans and a lightweight sweater, threw on one of her older trench coats, grabbed an umbrella and set out on foot, destination unknown. She'd brusquely told Irma she was taking a walk, which was precisely what she did, until even that tired her and she sank down on a park bench to watch the late afternoon pedestrians scurry between the raindrops.

She was bored. After all this time as Deanna Cauley Hunt, she was truly bored! For years she'd done the same things day in and day out, followed the same schedule week after week, month after month. Now, suddenly, she was bored.

Bored. Lonely. Frustrated. Restless. Was one any different from the next? Had this all been Mark's doing . . . or had eventual ennui been inevitable?

She wasn't sure how long she sat there with her umbrella shielding her from the world. Peering from beneath its scalloped edge, she studied the people passing and wondered what interesting lives they might lead. It was pure self-pity in which she indulged and she didn't feel an ounce of guilt. Sitting there half drenched in deck shoes, jeans and raincoat, she felt as if she'd attained a momentary measure of anonymity. It was delightful! In a burst of defiance she reached up, tore out the tortoiseshell clip that had held her hair, shook her head until the thick strands slithered freely down, then took a deep, satisfied breath. In a very strange way she'd never been so comfortable. And if her appearance shocked any of the hotel staff, who were so used to seeing her prim and proper . . . tough!

With a mutinous tilt to her chin she rose from the bench and made her way back to the Hunt International, more relaxed now and enjoying her willfulness. She even stopped to buy a chewy taffy bar, then proceeded to eat it—as no fine lady would—while she walked on through the rain, into the hotel lobby past doormen and bellboys and clerks to the elevator. It was a petty sort of rebellion, she smiled to herself as she licked the last of the chocolate from her well-manicured forefinger, but it did feel good! The smile was still on her face when she let herself into the suite, but it faded the instant she turned from the door. Mark!

"Where the devil have you been?" he yelled, striding from the living room at an angry pace. "I've been waiting for hours!"

Deanna caught sight of Irma in the background, but her main focus was Mark. "You haven't been waiting here for *hours*," she contradicted calmly. "I haven't been *gone* for hours."

"Where were you?" he repeated gratingly. "I've been worried sick!"

"You shouldn't have been. I was just taking a walk. Irma knew that."

"Taking a walk—all this time? And here I had the impression you spent Friday afternoons sitting at home. Do you have any idea how dangerous this city is, Deanna?"

His persistent anger surprised her. "It's broad daylight. There are people all over the place. I wasn't in any danger." Then she scowled, in part annoyed that her temporary good spirits had been dampened. "And why should *you* worry, anyway? It's been days since I've seen or heard from you. You sound as though we had a date arranged and I'd kept you waiting. Why *are* you here?" She paused to skim his lean frame. "And why are you dressed like that?" He wore well-worn jeans and a sweater of his own, topped by the denim jacket into which he now thrust his arms.

The hardness of his eyes didn't melt at all when he stepped forward, curved his fingers around her upper arm and turned her back toward the door. "I'm here to take you out. Let's go."

"Now wait a minute . . ." Deanna tried to free her arm but his grip only tightened. "What are you doing?"

He had the door open and paused only long enough

to call back over his shoulder, "Mrs. Hunt may not be in until late, Irma. Don't wait up for her. She'll be with me."

"Mark . . . !" Deanna lowered her voice out of habit when the door slammed shut and he led her down the corridor toward the elevator.

He too spoke in a more controlled voice now, deeper, somehow more dangerous, perversely exciting. "We're going out." He jabbed impatiently at the call button, but still didn't release her arm. "You're the one who's not a big talker, so I'll happily accommodate you for the time being. Besides, we wouldn't want to cause a ruckus. Wouldn't be very good for the image."

She heard his ridicule, felt its sting. But just when she would have lashed out in self-defense the elevator arrived. By the time it reached the lobby Mark's hold on her arm had slackened. Even in the muted silence of the populated elevator, he'd read her submission. For, despite her anger, her puzzlement, her hurt, she selfishly wanted to be with him. That was the bottom line. She'd never before been whisked away like this, almost by force, but not quite. It was another sort of fantasy, but one in which she knew her abductor, trusted him implicitly, was madly in love with him before the fact.

She reflected on this when she found herself seated several moments later in his deep blue Mercedes, waiting, watching as he slid behind the wheel, started the engine and took off without another glance her way. She felt as though she were headed for adventure and given her erstwhile boredom she couldn't deny the sense of exhilaration that slowly stole through her.

Or was it Mark? It always came down to that. Was Mark the be-all and end-all, the root of her ebullience? She cast him a surreptitious glance, then caught herself and boldly turned her head to stare at him. He was gorgeous. There was no other word to describe those devilishly dark good looks, dewy now from the moisture in the air and almost comically stern.

"What are you looking at?" he snapped, sparing a quick dark glance for her before returning his gaze to the road.

"You," she replied, feeling more gutsy, more brazen than she'd ever felt in her life. If this was an abduction she had every right to be indignant, even if its edge was a bit too soft for credibility. And since she'd already decided that she couldn't measure up to Mark's ideal, she had nothing to lose by being as outrageous as she wished. "Where are we going?" she demanded.

"You'll find out when we get there."

"Ah, such sweetness. Such concern for my peace of mind."

His hands tightened on the wheel, his strong knuckles turning pale. "Right now I'm concerned with my own peace of mind, Deanna. Now, will you keep still? I need to concentrate."

She followed his gaze to the rain-slickened road and realized for the first time that they were on Interstate 85, headed northeast of Atlanta. "Where are we going?" she murmured half to herself. When Mark didn't bother to answer she angled her head to the side and studied him again. "You know, you make a great ogre. You look terrific when you're angry."

He smiled. Crookedly. "So do you. You also look great with your hair wild like that. But I told you that before, didn't I? Finally decided to take my advice? Or did you do it just to torment me even more?"

"You're an egotist. I had no idea you'd be at my suite!" she cried, raising a hand to smooth her hair, sensing the futility of it, letting it fall back to her lap. "I really look a mess. It'll serve you right when we stop somewhere and people stare."

Mark offered a skeptical "Hmmmph!" but that was all. The rain had increased in force, so he turned away and switched the wipers to double time. Deanna settled back in her seat and peered through the rain-streaked window at the gently blurred rolling hills. There was something real yet unreal about the sight, much like the scene being played out in the car. It was diverting to a point, but as the minutes passed, the traffic thinned and the afternoon drew wearily toward evening, Deanna grew uneasy. Each minute took them farther from the familiarity of Atlanta.

"Mark, where are we going?"

"We're almost there."

"Is there a . . . restaurant in this neck of the woods?" She had assumed that the point of the jaunt was dinner out together, yet she could see nothing but the occasional turnoff and miles and miles of hilly, seemingly virgin forest. The highway was scenic even in the rain, winding up and around lakes, leading ever deeper into the mountains of northeast Georgia.

"Why? Are you hungry?" It was the first solicitous note he'd offered.

"A little."

"We'll be stopping in another twenty minutes or so."

Twenty minutes. Twenty miles. She grew more and more wary. The germ of a possibility darted through her mind, but she promptly ousted it. He wouldn't do that. . . .

But the signs all pointed to it when the stop he'd mentioned turned out to be a general store in a small blink-and-miss-it town in a pocket of the hills.

"Be right back," he murmured, climbing from the car and dashing through the rain to the store, returning within five minutes with a large brown bag in either arm, stowing them in the trunk before sliding into the driver's seat again.

Deanna watched him mop the rain from his forehead and proceed to unzip his jacket. Then, though the keys were in the ignition, he stretched to dig deep into the pocket of his jeans. When his hand emerged filled with change, she could stand no more.

"Mark . . . what's going on? Where are you taking me? What were those packages? And . . . what's that?" Her eyes were glued to his fingers, which had singled out a quarter and two dimes and now held them out to her.

*"That* is for a phone call."

With the premonition growing stronger, she raised her gaze to confront his. "And who is making a phone call?"

"You are."

"To . . . ?"

"To Irma."

Of course. Why had she even asked? She nodded as though a phone call had been part of the game plan all along. "That makes sense. 'Hello, Irma?' " she mimicked a possible conversation, " 'How's the weather down there?' " The look she turned on Mark was as dumb as she could make it.

Ironically her nonsense brought a softening to his features. "Come on, Deanna. I really don't need this. It's been one hell of a week for me and I'm exhausted. But the cabin doesn't have a telephone, so this is your last chance."

Not only did Deanna's eyes widen in understanding, but something deep inside lurched with Mark's fatigue. Whether he knew it or not, there was one sure-fire way of getting through to her.

Mark held her gaze while he finally revealed his intent. "I have a cabin another fifteen miles or so into the hills. I want you to call Irma and tell her that you won't be back in Atlanta until early Monday morning."

"Monday morning? That's the whole weekend . . ."

"Right."

"I can't do that, Mark!"

"Why not?"

Looking blindly out the window, she grasped at whatever came to mind. "For one thing, I've got other plans. Standing appointments tomorrow. A brunch on Sunday."

"Irma can cancel for you. She'll plead illness or . . . an emergency." He paused, visibly beginning to relax. "What else?"

Her attention fell to her jeans. "I haven't got any clothes—just these! No makeup. No comb or brush. Nothing!"

"You'll live without makeup. You don't need it anyway. And it wouldn't be the first time you've used my hairbrush. As for the clothes, there's a small washer and dryer at the cabin. Comes in handy."

*If you know how to use them.* Deanna scowled. "This is ridiculous! You can't just . . . kidnap me for the weekend."

"I can do anything I want. And so can you. This seemed to be the only way I knew of to teach you that!"

Feeling trapped, in part by a growing excitement at the prospect of having Mark to herself for an entire weekend, she mustered token resentment. "Now you've adopted my case?"

"It's my case too, Deanna. Don't forget that." *We'll be together,* he had whispered on that first momentous night. Just as his words then had given her courage, they did the same now. "Will you call?" she heard him ask, saw the coins still extended to her.

Her resistance lingered. "If I don't . . . ?"

Mark sighed, obviously having thought it all out in advance. "If you don't we'll have dinner at the cabin anyway and then I'll drive you home." Period. Done. Her choice. "I've brought you this far, but I can't force you to stay. You'll have to do that of your own free will."

When the action had been his—stealing her away from Atlanta, refusing to tell her their destination while the city fell farther and farther behind—it had been easy enough to accept. Now, however, he demanded her participation in the decision-making. She was momentarily beset by all the fears that had entered her life along with him.

"What did you have in mind for this weekend?" she asked more quietly, knowing he'd be able to read her timidity, unable to hide it.

He smiled his understanding. "Nothing terribly threatening. A quiet weekend. Sleep. Work around the cabin. Walks in the woods. I've got enough food to keep us stocked." He cocked his head back toward the trunk. "I phoned the order in this morning, so it was waiting. They're very accommodating."

Deanna ingested it all, seeing a threat where Mark saw none. She knew there had to be more, so she waited expectantly for him to elaborate, which he did in response to her silent question. His voice was lower, more gentle, so very much the Mark of her fantasy.

"Yes, I want that too. It's impossible for me to be with you without wanting to hold you, to touch you and make love to you. That's got to be part of the deal. If you can't accept it I'll drive you back to Atlanta."

She wanted to accept it, wanted desperately to feel his arms around her again. It was what she'd dreamed of, what had tormented her temptingly for days. But . . . what about after? Would he begin to pressure her again?

"It's for the weekend, Deanna. No more, no less. You give me your all for one weekend . . . and I'll drop you back at the Hunt International on Monday with nothing further said. It's as much as I can promise—one weekend with no strings attached. Anything later will be up to you."

Deanna pondered his proposal in silence. She considered the fears that loomed as large as ever. Should she agree to spend the weekend with Mark, he would have every opportunity to see exactly how inept a housemate she was. Should she *not* agree to the weekend, though, she might never forgive herself. It seemed too priceless to pass up, particularly since she'd been whisked away so quietly. Mark was right; Irma could cover for her. Her hair and nails would certainly survive. And as for the brunch . . . speaking of boredom . . .

That was the clincher. She didn't *want* to go back to that cocoon in which she'd been so restless all week. It was time to fly.

Her decision made, she took the change from him and let herself out of the car without another word. The phone booth was just outside the store. As she dialed and spoke to Irma, her eyes never left the shadowed figure waiting in the car, just as she knew he watched her. He had leaned across to open the door by the time she ran back, but he waited patiently for her to settle before he spoke.

"Well . . . ?" The one word embodied every last bit of his guardedness.

"She'll make my excuses," Deanna whispered, feeling shy as she stared out the front window. Then she bowed her head to concentrate on the hands clenched in her lap and fleetingly wondered if she'd made the right decision.

Mark didn't leave her to wonder long. Reaching over, he took her chin and raised her face to his, slid his hand around to circle her neck, then leaned forward. She knew he was going to kiss her, wanted him to. But he hesitated for an instant when he was still a breath away. Any lingering doubt in her mind was driven away by the warm caress of his eyes.

"Thank you." He sighed against her lips seconds before they opened for his kiss. It was deep and real, very different from the kisses of the past. In the confines of the small car under a Georgia mountain downpour there was no element of fantasy. Only life. True and rich. The gentle stroking of his lips, the soft brush of her own in return—these were full and honest in the way that life could be only at its most glorious moments. Deanna had made the decision, a commitment, and his reaction reflected it.

Easing his mouth from hers after a last reluctant sip, he pulled her beneath his arm, snug against his side. The Mercedes was soon on the road again.

Very slowly Deanna relaxed against his strength. Her initial awkwardness at having so shamelessly agreed to a weekend with him gradually ebbed away, a victim of the same recklessness that had motivated her earlier. It was clear that she would be her own greatest enemy if she spent the weekend worrying about a future without Mark once it was over. She realized that the only sensible course was to live for the moment, to enjoy the weekend without thoughts of beyond—as Mark appeared willing to do. She fit so comfortably at his side. As though agreeing, he squeezed her closer.

It was quite dark when they turned off the main road and commenced a series of twists and turns that were all the scarier in light of the weather. Deanna found herself sitting straighter and unconsciously squinting to see out the window, wanting to help him find the way. Mark, meanwhile, put both hands on the wheel.

"You've got a great sense of direction," she exclaimed. "I can't see a single marker for the life of me. How do you ever find your way?"

He laughed, a mellow sound from deep in his chest that pleased her with its obvious enjoyment of her awe. "I've come here too often to forget. I could almost do it in my sleep. Come to think of it, there were times when I came close."

"Sleep? It is a long drive. How often are you up here?"

"Once or twice a month for weekends. Longer stretches for vacations now and again."

"You drive all the way from Savannah each time?"

He cleared his throat in self-mockery. "I've taken small planes several times, but . . . I'm not much of a flier."

"You're kidding! A man of the world like you? You've got to fly if you work in all those different states."

"What I *have* to do, I do. When it comes to business, you're right. I have to fly. When it comes to pleasure, though, I prefer the wheel in my hands and the pedals under my own feet. Besides, a jumbo jet to Des Moines or St. Louis is one thing. A rubber-band hamlet-hopper is another."

She grinned. "Well put. But the ride must be tedious, coming up here over and over again."

"Not really." He took another sharp turn, then straightened out. Deanna couldn't identify much beyond the headlights' beams and gave up the watch. "I do some of my best thinking during the drive. It's usually very relaxing."

His emphasis on the "usually" provoked her in a good-humored sort of way. "And it's not now?"

"The weather, Deanna. My preference is for nice dry daylight. This is a little soupy for my taste."

She followed his sharpened gaze. "Well . . . where *is* this cabin of yours?"

"Coming. Coming. Be patient."

Two more twists and a gentle curve brought them over a rough road into a clearing. Deanna could still see nothing and might not even have known they'd arrived had the car not come to a smooth stop.

"We're here?"

"We're here."

She leaned forward. "I can't see a thing, Mark!" In the pitch blackness she could make out nothing but large shapes and she would have been hard-pressed to say where forest ended and house began or vice versa.

"Then you'll just have to trust me to get you safely

inside, won't you?" Mark growled, playful for the first time that day.

"I guess so." She feigned resignation, but the eagerness with which she slid from the car belied her tone. Mark took her hand and led her on up the curved path toward what she now saw to be a building, large in its own right, yet still dwarfed by the surrounding fortress of evergreens.

"Watch your step," he warned softly, tightening his grip on her hand when she nearly stumbled on a misplaced stone. "Looks like the rain's done a job out here. I'll have to see to that in the morning."

They ran up several steps to the cover of a broad overhang, where Mark dropped her hand to unlock the door and shove it open, reached back to usher her inside, then left her standing in the darkness while he crossed the room and fumbled with several switches. The steady patter of rain on the roof almost muffled the hum of the independent generator. In less than a minute, however, the lights flickered on.

"Let me get the things from the car," he suggested in passing. "I'll be right back."

He dashed out so quickly that she wondered if he'd purposely left her alone to appraise his home for the first time. Could he actually have doubted that she'd like it? Gasping in pleasure, she grew more and more enchanted as she slowly perused the view. It was a work of architectural genius, a home like none she'd ever seen before. If she'd expected a rustic, rough-hewn mountain retreat, she had totally underestimated his taste, not to mention his unbelievable talent. This home could have been a showpiece in any urban setting, yet he'd chosen to hide it away from the world for his appreciation alone. And now hers.

Turning her head for a more leisurely examination, she finally began to assimilate what she saw. The first and overall impression had been of a cultured grandeur. Her closer scrutiny broke the house down into each of its component parts.

From the warmth and dryness of the interior, Deanna saw what she'd been unable to see from outside. The house was predominantly round, its huge front living area taking up two-thirds of a circle. Its walls were wood, as in any traditional cabin, but these planks ran vertically rather than horizontally and were smoothed and treated to give a fine finished ash-blond veneer. Near the back the break in the circular pattern allowed for two variations. The first was in the form of a kitchen, spaciously square and neatly integrated into the whole by a cleanly banded archway. The second was more enclosed, more private. Its door stood ajar, revealing it to be a bedroom.

Deanna wasn't quite sure what drew her boldly forward to that room, whether it was the roof of the house with its steady upward slant as it spread back or whether it was the subtle thread of anticipation within herself. She moved quietly, oblivious to Mark's return and the sound of his footsteps headed toward the kitchen.

She was utterly captivated. Before her was a room as sparsely furnished and decorated as the other, with nothing but the elegance of simplicity to enhance its flavor. There was the bed. Freestanding, not far from the back wall, it was bounded on all four sides by two tiers of steps, thickly carpeted, as was all the flooring in this room. The bed was a throne, an altar. High above it the ceiling reached its apex, its slant embedded with vast skylights that transmitted the spatter of rain rather than the twinkle of stars. She felt as though she were part of the elements, yet she was safely sheltered and warm within.

Indulging in a final moment's awe, she turned and half ran to the kitchen, stopping short on its threshold to see Mark very calmly and quietly storing groceries.

"Mark!" she breathed, unable to contain her excitement even when he looked up so soberly. "It's fantastic!"

He finished placing a tin of coffee on the shelf, closed the cabinet and turned to her. "You like it?"

"Like it? It's magnificent! How could I possibly *not* like it?"

"You could very easily hate it if you resented my having brought you here. It may not be quite as fancy as what you're used to . . ."

His unsureness took her aback, but only for a minute. "I love it! I've never seen anything so . . . so naturally compatible with its setting!"

"Wait till you see it tomorrow. In the light of day there's a different feeling still." Midway through the expression of his pride, his voice caught. "You . . . are staying, aren't you? Haven't changed your mind or gotten cold feet?"

She shook her head and offered him a hushed assurance. "No. I haven't changed my mind. I'll stay."

"For the whole weekend?"

Touched by his softness, she stared at him. So tall and strong, independent and established, he seemed suddenly vulnerable again, depending on her as no one had ever done. Perhaps if she'd had a child to give of herself to, her protective instinct might have been slaked. But she had no child, could have no child. And she desperately wanted Mark to need her.

Something in her chest swelled, choking off sound from her throat. Covering the short distance between them, she slid her arms around his waist and laid her head on his chest, pulling herself warmly against the full length of him. She heard his heartbeat, felt the muscles of his back flex at her touch. With a low groan of acknowledgment he completed the circle, engulfing her in his own embrace, but only briefly.

"Here, Deanna," he said, setting her back and reaching out to help her. "Let me have your coat. It's wet. I'll give you the formal tour and then we can make something to eat. You did tell me you were hungry, didn't you?"

*That* was when she'd assumed they'd be stopping at a restaurant. Now, with the impending exposure of her culinary ignorance, she wasn't quite sure.

"Uh, I'm all right now. It passed."

"Yours, perhaps . . . but come on. Let me show you around."

As she'd half suspected, there was scarcely a convenience not deftly camouflaged behind one panel or another in the main room, which had a central pit consisting of endlessly connected sofa sections, a side work area with a drafting table and high chair, a bar, small stereo and multitudinous book shelves. Deanna guessed that there was a good foot and a half between the outer wall and this inner one to accommodate the storage space.

Similarly, in the bedroom, though there appeared to be no major furniture other than the bed, Mark revealed hidden drawers, closets and even a door she hadn't previously detected, which led to a bathroom. It, too, she was to discover, was modern and well appointed.

"Everything is so clean," she marveled, stunned again by the difference between this and the stereotypical log cabin.

Mark chuckled as he led her full circle back to the kitchen. "That's because it's unused for days on end. And because everything's hidden behind panels. Dust can't begin to collect on what it can't reach. I hate cleaning." *So do I,* she mused apprehensively, but said nothing as she sensed a more immediate dilemma. "Okay!" He looped his thumbs into the back pockets of his jeans and her pulse raced at the tautened pull across his hips. "How about steak, fresh string beans and baked potatoes?"

Her pulse continued to race and she wasn't sure what to do about the dilemma. "Sounds fine." She nodded, feeling decidedly fraudulent. She stood by watching as Mark extracted one ingredient after another from the refrigerator and set them on the counter. How difficult could it be—preparing this simple meal?

"How about if you prepare the beans while I put the potatoes in? They take the longest."

"Prepare the beans," she echoed him, keeping her mockery well in check. How dumb could she be? Why hadn't she ever gone in to give Irma a hand with dinner? How could she be so totally helpless? Prepare the beans. Fine. But what to do first . . . ?

"Something wrong?"

Her head snapped up and she found Mark staring at her warily. He'd guessed! What would he think of her now? She couldn't hide the self-disgust that spread across her features. But self-disgust turned to dismay when his tone chilled, then to astonishment when he spoke.

"I'm sorry, Deanna, but they don't have maid service in this neck of the woods. I know that the thought of doing for yourself must be a new one, and if it's so reprehensible, I apologize. But it's either chip in or go without."

There was no possible way Mark could have known the hours upon hours of agonizing she'd done on the issue of her lack of experience, much less the extent of her embarrassment now. Therefore he was astonished in his turn by what appeared on the surface to be an unwarranted outburst and was actually the culmination of those long hours of worry.

"Reprehensible?" Eyes wide, she took a step back as if warding off his anger. "The only thing that's at all reprehensible is *your* lack of faith." Hurt, she barreled on. "I'd be glad to do whatever there is to be done—if only I knew how! Do you think I like to feel stupid . . . or helpless?" In the turmoil of her confession, she was unaware of his dawning understanding. Even the softening of his features was beyond her notice.

"I've never been put in this position in my entire life," she ranted on, "and believe me, it's mortifying! If I could snap my fingers and magically turn into a French chef I would! I'd like nothing better than to cook you the most beautiful dinner. . . ." Her words were drowned out by his hearty guffaw. "And what's so funny?" She literally shook with humiliation and could only hope she wouldn't cry, though perversely, that was what she wanted more than anything to do. Crawl into a corner and bawl. Granted, there wasn't an overabundance of corners in this house. . . .

"Deanna, Deanna . . ." His laughter died down as he reached out and hauled her against him. She resisted, holding her body rigid.

"You're laughing at me."

"You bet I am! That's about the fieriest I've ever seen you. And with such a confession!"

"You're laughing at me."

"No, honey. That's relief you hear. For a minute I thought you *were* horrified at the idea of helping make dinner. It was wrong of me, I know, but that look of absolute disgust on your face . . ."

"I'm disgusted with myself!"

"But *I* didn't know that. It's your own fault for not having confided in me before. Why couldn't you just say that you didn't know how to cook?"

She began to feel the beginnings of her own relief. "I feel ridiculous, Mark! What kind of woman has never cooked a meal?"

He held her back to look at her. "A woman who's

140

never *had* to. Most women would give anything to be in your shoes. To have never had occasion to cook—that's their greatest fantasy."

"Some fantasy," she snorted as she buried her face against his chest. He smelled manly and divine and she was suddenly light-headed. At least now he *did* know and he wasn't terribly disappointed. Perhaps she'd done him a disservice all along by assuming he wouldn't understand.

"Any more true confessions?" he asked in a deep drawl.

Giddy as she felt, Deanna sensed that there wouldn't be a better time. Her eyes apologized in advance. "I've never done the laundry or cleaned the bathroom. And I couldn't brew a pot of coffee if my life depended on it. My hair may well be unmanageable without its usual Saturday conditioning. And without a manicure my fingernails will go progressively downhill. But"—she paused, lapsing into a sweet singsong—"don't tell me I didn't warn you."

Mark smiled and shook his head. "What you don't seem to realize is that those things don't matter to me, particularly up here. That's one of the reasons I wanted to bring you. There's no social pressure here. Just you and me. And besides"—his eyes took on a familiar gleam—"by Monday morning I intend to see a very healthy flush on your cheeks. Between the fresh outdoors . . . and the wild indoors . . . see, there it is, starting already!"

"You're impossible!" She forced out a scowl, blushing all the more.

"I'm also hungry. Come on." He swung her to his side and brought her back to the counter. "Lesson number one. Snapping string beans."

# 8

~~~~~~~~~~~~~~~

**D**inner was as delicious a meal as Deanna had ever eaten, though with the weight of one giant burden lifted from her shoulders she would have devoured almost anything edible.

"And you said you weren't hungry," Mark kidded her later as they sat side by side in the living room with soft music in the background, brandy snifters in their hands, contentment in the air.

"I'm really ashamed to say that I never worked in the kitchen with Irma," she began, her tongue loosened by the heady combination of Mark and brandy. "She was always there. She usually took her time off when I had plans to go out. And on the rare occasion that I was in the suite without her I only had to call room service."

"Some life . . ."

"I suppose."

"What about before you married?"

"The same thing. The cook we had when I was a child

wouldn't *let* us into the kitchen. It was her own private domain. I'm sure I could have been more insistent but . . . well . . . I never had cause to insist."

"You don't have to make excuses, Deanna."

"But I do. I feel absurd!"

"You just prepared a lovely meal."

"*You* prepared the meal. I just followed your instructions. Where did you learn all you know, anyway?"

"Self-made, self-taught. Actually, it was pure survival. Don't forget that I've been a bachelor for years. I like home cooking and there are many times when I simply don't have the patience to wait for a meal in a restaurant. I never go in for anything fancy, just enough to keep flesh on the bones."

"Some flesh!" She poked playfully at his ribs and was rewarded when he dragged her under his arm. He made no attempt to kiss her, seeming content simply to hold her, and she had no complaint. Bare feet curled beneath her, she in turn curled against Mark. His strong arm curved around her shoulder, then back across her chest. She was in heaven.

"Tell me about your life, Mark."

"My life?" He roused himself from his own relaxed trance to echo the words.

"You know . . . what you do everyday."

"I work."

She felt him nestle his cheek more comfortably against the crown of her head. "And . . . ?"

"And come home."

"That's all? Work and come home?"

"Usually." He sounded exhausted. "I lead a quiet existence."

Glancing across him, she saw that he'd finished his brandy. His words weren't slurred though, simply unhurried. "What do you do for fun?"

"For fun? Work is fun. And I putter around building

things of my own. You know, improving things, renovating."

"Did you build this place *yourself?*"

"Almost . . . but not quite. I had help."

"It's fantastic, Mark. You must be so proud!"

"I enjoy it." He paused to think. "You know, I think if I had my choice I'd be a carpenter. *There's* a feeling of pride!"

"Why don't you . . . be a carpenter?"

He chuckled. "Ah, the voice of the secure speaking." His warm squeeze precluded offense. "Actually, when I reach my third million I may consider it!"

Deanna indulged herself with the image of living with Mark in the mountains forever while he built homes on the nearby peaks. It was a lovely dream, though dangerous. "Tell me about your home in Savannah," she demanded, needing to escape the image. "Is it modern like this?"

"Not quite." He smiled. "It's a beautiful old house on a beautiful old street. When I bought it I tore out the insides and I've done it over little by little since. It's almost complete." His voice slowed, then faded.

"Sounds nice."

"Ummm."

"You really love your work, don't you?"

"Ummm."

She angled her head so she could see his face. "Either you've run out of words . . . or you really are tired."

Eyelids that had been closed lifted heavily. "I'm tired. It *was* a horrid week. Then, driving from Savannah to Atlanta and pacing the floors at your place for hours . . ."

"It wasn't hours."

"Well, it seemed it. I was worried. From what Irma said, you don't usually just up and take off like that."

"I don't usually just up and take off like *this* either!"

"This is different. And you had an accomplice. Anyway, it's been a very long day. Now, with you here in my arms, finally, all to myself—"

"Boring you so much that you're falling asleep—"

"You're not boring me. I'm very, very content."

Deanna felt the same way. Strange—now that they were alone, with all the freedom in the world, the only thing that mattered was sitting close like this. Anything more would shatter the beauty of the moment.

"Deanna?" he murmured groggily.

"Hmmm?"

"Is it all right . . . I mean, would you mind . . . could we go to bed . . . to sleep . . . ?"

It was scary. He had to have read her mind. As many times as it had happened, it still amazed her. Soulmates. She'd always thought so.

"That'd be fine, Mark," she whispered. "You're beat." Slipping from him, she took the glass from his hand and brought both it and her own to the kitchen sink, where she rinsed them and set them upside down to dry. When she returned to the living room he wasn't there. A rummaging sound from the bedroom caught her attention and she padded toward it.

Mark had opened one of the panels to stand before a tall set of drawers, one of which was open and in the process of being rifled. "Ahhh," he muttered in satisfaction when he drew a particular shirt from the drawer, closed everything up, then turned to Deanna. "Here. My best red-flannel backyard logger's shirt. I knew it was here somewhere. It's the softest I've got." At her blank look he explained. "Your nightgown."

She smiled, embarrassed. "That's right. I don't seem to have anything else, do I?"

"My fault, I'm afraid. This is the least I can do." He paused. "Would you like a shower?"

"Mmmm."

He tilted his auburn head toward the bathroom. "There are plenty of towels and extra supplies in the cabinet to the left of the sink. I'll wait until you're done." He smiled sleepily and she wondered if he'd make it that long.

"Are you sure you wouldn't like to go first?"

He shook his head. "Go on. I'll just lie down and wait my turn." When he turned around to do just that she acceded.

Rushing was no easy task in that luxurious backwoods bathroom, particularly given her own state of languor. She reveled in the hot spray for a blissful eternity, even deciding to wash her hair, no matter how it turned out. The supplies Mark had mentioned had turned out to include a bonanza of personal items that he must have had thrown in with the groceries that afternoon. By the time she emerged from the bathroom fresh and clean, her hair still damp but not half as bad as she'd expected and Mark's red plaid shirt buttoned down to her thighs, Mark was sound asleep.

She stood immobilized for several minutes, a step inside the bedroom, as a wave of pure adoration swept over her. He had bothered only to draw back the almond-and-brown-striped quilt before stretching out on the sheets and surrendering to exhaustion. He lay on his stomach fully dressed, one arm bent up behind his head, the other flung out in front of his face.

Deanna inched forward, feeling her love swell. It was an effort to keep her pulse steady as she mounted the steps and sank onto the bed close beside him.

"Mark?" she murmured. Much as she hated to do it, she gently shook his shoulder. "Mark? Shouldn't you get undressed?" He struggled to open his eyes without success. "Mark?" she whispered again. "Mark?" He was obviously dead to the world, his breathing deep and even.

Acting purely on instinct and without further thought, she inched his sweater up over his back and nudged him over. His only response was a muffled grunt. When she waited a moment and he still didn't waken, she assumed that he was safely beyond disturbing.

She undressed him quietly, pulling the sweater higher, then dragging each arm from its sleeve and lifting his head to ease the pullover off. His shirt was a simpler matter, easily unbuttoned and dispensed with. On the pretense of resting she paused for a moment's perusal of his chest. Its even rise and fall mesmerized her. She reached out to touch the dark feathered hazing there, but halted her hand just above it before tracing the tapering line to the snap of his jeans.

Sighing, she shimmied the denim down over his legs and off his bare feet. Then she grinned helplessly as she saw all that remained. All? The devil . . . he must have planned this from the start! Her gaze flew to his face, thoroughly expecting to encounter his fully awake and mischievous regard. But his dark lashes rested at the rugged height of his cheekbone and his face bore nothing but the sweet pleasure of sleep.

Satisfied that he wasn't mocking her she dared to focus again on the one item of clothing in which she'd let him sleep. And again she grinned. Red! Red briefs this time! Slung low on his hips, fitting him to perfection. His bottoms to her tops—the red coordinated perfectly.

She sat still for a minute, thinking how very much she loved him, how very happy she was to be there with him. Right now that *other* life was the unreal one, a world away and totally irrelevant. This place and Mark were the only things that mattered.

Leaning over his feet, she freed the quilt and pulled it

up to cover them as she stretched out beside him. It was at this moment, when the bed was finally still, that Mark stirred.

"Deanna . . .?" he moaned, seeming to return from a far dream to call her.

"I'm here," she whispered, letting herself be drawn back against him.

"You'll stay?" He seemed more asleep than awake.

"I'll stay." She snuggled in more closely.

"Good," he mumbled, then tightened his hold and offered a barely audible "I love you" against her hair before his breathing resumed the even cadence of sleep.

"I love you too." She mouthed the words, knowing he couldn't hear and suspecting his confession to have been nothing more than grogginess speaking. There were so many things that seemed out of reach—a future together, even a family. If only she could give Mark a child with that same full head of auburn hair and those warm brown eyes—but enough! It was best to simply enjoy what she did have.

She fell asleep in a haze of contentment and awoke to the morning sun and Mark's melting gaze. He was propped up on an elbow, savoring every minute of her slow arousal.

"Good morning, sleepyhead," he murmured softly.

"Same to you." She echoed the greeting as the events—or nonevents—of the evening before returned to her mind.

"Sleep well?" he asked.

She stretched and smiled contentedly. "Uh-huh. And you?"

He nodded, skimming the length of the shirt she wore. "You look great."

She felt shy, though it also felt totally natural to awaken in Mark's bed. "So do you." Reaching spontaneously toward his hair, she combed a wave back from his forehead. He caught first his breath, then her hand, taking it down to his lips to press her fingers there. His eyes held hers, beaming their heat into her, sending a privately coded message. Further tingles erupted along her nerve ends when he singled out her slender pinkie and sensuously sucked it.

There in the mountains they were free, stripped of the trappings of civilization. There would be no worries there, no interruptions. Deanna felt light-headed and very much in love. And the near nudity of Mark's body deeply stirred her.

She heard his name on her lips, repeated softly again and again until his mouth swallowed all sound. Reaching up to luxuriate in the rich thickness of his hair, she held him ever closer. He kissed her breathless and she was swept along, clinging to him through the realization that he was in so many ways the source of her strength. He'd given her so much, taught her so much more. With him she was a new person.

She allowed him to ease her back down on the bed and submitted to the heat of his touch as he carefully unbuttoned her shirt and slowly spread it open. He regarded her body with a kind of reverence and she knew the pride of his satisfaction. If she'd ever worried that he wouldn't be pleased, that doubt was erased now. He might have been unveiling a collection of priceless jewels and she felt prized indeed.

When his hands followed his gaze in a sensual exploration of her feminine contours she rejoiced in his softly erotic words of praise. When she moved against him in search of more he fell back, bringing her over on top of him. What commenced then was an interlude of frenzied involvement, an intense entanglement of bodies that reflected every minute of the long days and even longer nights since they'd last made love. Deanna returned everything Mark gave and he gave fiercely. They were on his territory now and he took full initiative.

She was convinced that he shared the sense of freedom she felt in his house in the woods, because he read her perfectly. There was no timidity in her now, barely even the last remnants of shyness. He sensed her growing comfort with herself as a woman of passion and felt that much more comfortable challenging her to greater heights, which he did in new and wonderfully tender ways.

Deanna knew that she was in paradise. When she found herself lying suddenly on her back again she gazed past Mark's head at the wispy canopy of green high above the skylight. The sun and wind played through the branches to cast exotic patterns on the panes.

As though part of nature himself, Mark moved with similar grace while his mouth did fantastic things to her body. She felt the fragments of flame he left behind with each touch—the gentle sucking of her nipple; the roll of his tongue just below her navel; the nip of his teeth on the skin of her inner thigh. By the time she restlessly coaxed him to peel the red briefs from his hips he was as much on fire as was she. Her fingers teased him as his did her until she writhed in sweet agony beneath him, longing for his total possession.

It came with a glorious thrust that brought a throaty cry of ecstasy. "Ahhhh . . . Mark . . . you feel so good!"

"Kiss me, Deanna," he moaned, and she did. She offered him every bit of the love she felt, let it explode through their many touchpoints as her lips opened to his, her hands kneaded the muscles of his lower back, her hips arched in timely counterpoint to his.

She put every bit of her soul into the act of pleasing him and she was a blinding success. Mark cried out her name and stiffened, then was unable to hold off any longer. His body shuddered and reverberated with quiet aftershocks until he finally collapsed on top of her.

"I'm sorry, honey. I'm sorry. I—I lost control," he panted. "That hasn't happened in years." His arms tightened around her back. "I'm sorry."

But Deanna wasn't. She felt a distinct sense of victory. "Was it good?" she asked, smiling with pride and feminine satisfaction. The bodily anticipation that remained within her was secondary to the knowledge of what she'd done.

Mark's head was buried against her neck. "Oh, Deanna, you know it was." As if in further proof she felt lingering tremors snake their way through his limbs. "See what you do to me?" He raised his head to offer the grinning accusation. At the moment when she felt his weight begin to crush her he levered himself up on his forearms. "It's damned embarrassing is what it is!"

She cocked her head skeptically. "What is?"

"To lose control like that. Every man wants to see himself as the perfect lover. You know—endless stamina, ultimate self-control. I guess I blew the image."

"Am I complaining?" she kidded him softly, suddenly all too aware of the brush of her breasts against his chest with each breath.

"You're too polite." He returned her good-humored banter, seemingly ignorant of the titillating connection, perhaps simply sated.

But she grew serious. "That's not it at all, Mark. You have no idea how good I feel to know that I can arouse you to the extent that you'd lose that practiced control. It's a real ego trip, especially for someone like me who . . ."

She couldn't finish, but Mark understood. "Who never saw herself in the role of the tigress?"

She blushed. "I wouldn't have chosen quite that word, but . . . that's the idea."

"You *are* a tigress when you let go, Deanna." He caressed her with his hushed tones. "I've never been as satisfied . . . or as insatiable."

His words brought her eyes up sharply and she felt him move again deep inside her. She hadn't expected this. "Mark?" she whispered, coming alive herself with a matching fire.

Mark lowered his head, then ran his tongue lightly and sensuously over the curve of her upper lip. She closed her eyes to savor the sensation, opened her lips to deepen it.

"Let go for me, honey. I need you," he rasped. Then, with paired thrusts, he plunged his tongue into her mouth and moved his hips against hers until she had no choice but to yield to the joyful onslaught.

This time Mark was the epitome of control, the masterful lover he had wanted to be. Time and again he brought her to the edge of insanity, only to pull her back and temper her passion until he was ready to lead her onward once more. He seemed determined to show her a new world of divine plateaus, each one higher and hotter than the last, each one mind-bending. Even her strained pleas for release couldn't dent his purpose. He brought her out of her shell—permanently—demolishing the last shreds of her cocoon, turning her not into an elusive butterfly but the very tigress he'd claimed her to be. She responded to him with wild abandon, engulfed in the rapture of love.

Finally she gasped and cried out, then clung to him while her body was seized by endless spasms. Only then did Mark allow for his own release, joining her in explosive ecstasy, exulting with her at that topmost plateau of gratification before slowly, reluctantly returning to earth.

Deanna lay suspended in a state of near shock. She'd never in her life experienced anything as powerful as the quakes that surged more quietly now between her body and Mark's and back. The force had been the intimate declaration of two people united in every possible sense. It had been a magnificent moment, a moment far beyond fantasy, a moment that seemed the ultimate justification of her existence. In that moment's explosion she and Mark had produced something far more than the simple sum of their parts. Should she never experience it again, Deanna knew its remembered glory would always be with her.

"What is it, Deanna?" She heard Mark's worried murmur and opened her eyes with a jolt to find them flooded with tears.

Smiling, she buried her face against his chest when he rolled from her onto his side. "It was so beautiful," she whispered breathlessly. "So very beautiful."

Untrusting of his own voice, Mark kissed the wetness from her cheeks and held her tightly. He spoke only when she had quieted. "Well . . . what do you think?" he asked, releasing her only far enough to view her face.

"About what?"

"Breakfast. You've been such a, uh, smashing success at this, are you up for taking a crack at eggs?"

"That's not the issue," she countered pertly.

"No?"

"No. The issue is whether you're up for eating the eggs I crack!"

They'd set the tone for the morning, indeed, for the entire day. Fortunately, the eggs he ordered were scrambled, and with Mark calling the shots over her shoulder she managed to turn them out moist onto waiting plates. He'd taken care of the rest—juice and country ham, cornbread and coffee—but she felt pleased nonetheless and eager to tackle more another time.

They spent the better part of the day working together

around the house, Mark at the helm, Deanna his ready assistant. He conscientiously gave her her share of work, patiently demonstrating each particular chore, allowing for her mistakes, beaming his pride when she succeeded.

"I don't know how you've done without my help all these years," she mocked herself, able to do so now that she felt a growing self-confidence. They'd just finished clearing the front path of the scattering of loose stones washed down by the rain. And before that they'd painted a sealer on the fresh pine of the raised rear deck. "To think that my skills have been wasted for so long!" she exclaimed.

The day had grown progressively warmer. In the mid-afternoon heat Deanna mopped perspiration from beneath the heavy fall of hair on her neck. Instead of the sweater she'd arrived in she wore another of Mark's shirts, a lightweight short-sleeved job which she had rakishly knotted just above her waist.

As for Mark, he'd long since shucked his shirt completely. His torso gleamed beneath its damp sheen of sweat. Unable to resist what was to her true masculinity, she reached out and stroked the hard-corded curve of his shoulder.

"What was *that* for?" he growled, drawing her flush against him. His fingers deftly infiltrated her waistband and pressed insistently at the small of her back until she felt the steel of his thighs against her own.

"Just feeling my oats," she teased.

"*Your* oats? Or *my* shoulder?"

"Same difference. I would never have dared to just reach out and touch a man like that before."

"You never touched Larry that way?"

She stiffened and tried to move, but he held her firmly. "That's unfair, Mark."

"It's not unfair. Simply a question. You've got to learn not to feel uncomfortable referring to Larry. What you had with him through nine years of marriage was something pretty special. What we've got is pretty special, too, but as different from that as night from day. That our relationship is a more passionate one is no reflection on the quality of your marriage to Larry. There are so many things he gave you that I can't begin to give. But I like to feel that I give you something he never did."

"You do," she whispered, eyes glued to the strong features above her. "You must know that by now."

His slanted grin touched her heart. "I guess I need that reassurance once in a while."

To further reassure him she leaned forward to kiss his chest, drawing moist patterns with her tongue around one tiny raised nub. Her hands sampled the damp smoothness at his sides, running up and down their naked length until he begged for mercy.

"I was wrong, Deanna. *You're* the insatiable one around here!" he declared in a wicked drawl. With trembling arms he set her back, then grabbed her hand and led her forward. "Come on. Let's take a walk! There's a super brook not far from here."

He led her carefully through the forest, holding branches out of her way, weaving their way between trees, passing over and around low-growing ferns and grasses on a path she couldn't for the life of her see. Her curiosity grew as they walked on, saying nothing to each other because the beauty of the idyllic scene said it all on its own. As had been the case the night before, he knew his way perfectly. And as had been the case the night before, the destination was well worth the trek.

Deanna found herself at the most beautiful, most secluded spot she'd ever seen. Even more than the clearing back at the house, this setting moved her. It was pure and untouched.

Her eyes widened to take in the rich greenery all about, the dance of sun and the whisper of wind through branches that reached ever upward, verdant ladders to the sky. She smelled the ripe aroma of the fall and listened to the rustle of nature's creatures in the undergrowth. But the brook had to be the central jewel in the cluster. Smooth and sparkling, its narrow span opened to a wider, deeper swirl before narrowing again and disappearing around a bend.

"It's wonderful!" Deanna breathed, only then turning her glittering gaze to Mark.

He stood close by her side, hands on his hips, enjoying her appreciation. A brilliant smile, the likes of which he gave on only very special occasions, burst out. "I thought you'd like it. This has to be my favorite spot. I come here at least once per trip to sit, to think, to swim . . ." His hands moved to the snap of his jeans.

"What are you doing?" she said in a hoarse stage whisper, and he replied in mocking kind.

"Going swimming."

"Mark . . .?"

"Yeeees . . .?"

"We haven't got suits."

"We don't need them. There's no one here but us and Him"—his eyes shot heavenward—"and He's seen it all before." He'd waded into the brook and submerged himself at its deepest point before Deanna realized the absurdity of her modesty, not to mention the conspiratorial whisper she'd maintained quite subconsciously. It was small solace to say she'd been driven by habit. Mark was right. A bathing suit was unnecessary here.

Much as she tried, however, she couldn't help but feel self-conscious when she took off her own clothes and gingerly tested the water. Mark watched her every step, ensuring her safety as he enjoyed the view.

"Atta girl," he crooned, extending a hand to her as she sought the footing with which he was so naturally familiar. She caught his fingers and let him tow her to the deepest spot. Then, with the water buoying her, she wrapped her arms about his neck.

"Now this is luxury!" she cried softly, referring to the invigorating chill of the brook, but sharply aware that the interpretation she gave the term was a new one for her.

"Ummm. I'll say." He murmured his agreement suggestively, circling her back and bringing her body into intimate contact with his.

Deanna lowered her voice playfully. "Why do I sense we're talking about different things?"

He nipped at the soft lobe of her ear. "Are we?" His hands fell lower and she began to understand. Luxury *was* relative. There was the world of material luxury in which she'd been born and bred, into which she'd married, in which she still lived. And there was the natural luxury of the mountains, the virgin goodness of the land that harbored them.

Yet this was no less a luxury—the hardness of Mark's lean body supporting hers, rising against hers. She felt his hands at the back of her thighs and yielded to their gentle pressure, twining her legs around his hips, coiling her arms more tightly around his neck. When he kissed her she was ready; when he touched her she stirred his heat in turn; when he slowly and sensually fitted himself to her she experienced the greatest luxury of all.

The fullness of love. Physical. Emotional. Though unspoken, it was felt. Deanna had to believe that in those precious moments it existed. As surely as the sun warmed the brook, so their love glittered and grew, exploding at last in a moment she could barely recall when she found herself lying on the shore sometime later.

Mark had spread her shirt on the mossy bed, then laid her gently atop. He sat by her side. "To sit, to think, to swim . . . to make love. I've always wanted to do that."

She grinned shyly. "You do it very well. Of course, I'm still a novice at outdoor acrobatics."

"Stick around and I'll show you more," he rejoined smartly, then realized that he hadn't been so smart after all. Her facial expression had tightened instantly. There was still Monday to face, not to mention all the days after.

To compensate for his blunder he kissed her, kept her preoccupied with inane prattle on the mating habits of the blue-tailed muskrat while he took exaggerated pains in dressing her, dressed himself with no pain at all and led her home. She was more than happy to quash all thought of the future, unwilling to let tomorrow rain on today's parade.

For the most part she was successful. It was only occasionally that a statement triggered her silent alarm or a look turned heartrendingly poignant. At those times Deanna would think of love and the future, of a happiness she would never know and a child certain not to be. When they made love again on Sunday morning, this time in the bright sunshine on the enclosed back deck, there was a fierceness to it that heralded their upcoming separation.

But there was something else, too. Deanna had spent the last two weeks, the past two days, gaining confidence in herself as a woman. At last she believed in her ability to please Mark sexually. And for the first time she believed in her right as a woman to enjoy her womanhood. Mixed with the fierceness of their lovemaking was that new-found confidence plus a sense of adventure that would have positively shocked her in her "other" life.

Later she was to reflect on that particular morning and sizzle all over again. The fact that she'd ventured to sunbathe in the nude had been enough out of character to make her blush.

"I'll have you know that I don't usually do this," she'd warned Mark at the start. They had just showered together and neither wore more than a terry towel knotted appropriately.

"I don't know why not," he kidded her.

She'd taken the bait. "It's this funny thing about living in a hotel in the middle of the city. Exhibitionism just wouldn't do."

He had taken a pair of air mattresses from the storage area beneath the deck and bent to push them side by side. He turned to squint up at the sun and adjusted the mats accordingly. "There. These have really come in handy."

"You sunbathe often?" she asked, but knew the answer already. She was familiar with every nuance of his body. When he casually dropped his towel to reveal an even expanse of tanned flesh she wasn't surprised. Nonetheless, her own tingled.

"Here? Yup." Spreading the towel out, he eased himself down, then stretched straight out on his back and closed his eyes. "Actually, I've used the mattresses even more often at night."

"At night? Not sunbathing." She laughed, sinking to her knees on her own mattress.

"Nope . . . sleeping."

"Here? Outside?"

"Uh-huh. The summer nights are often beautiful. Cool. Clear. Peaceful."

"Sounds heavenly."

"It is."

She stretched out beside him, only then tugging open her towel and letting it fall to either side. "How about the winter. Do you come here then?" Closing her eyes, she was aware for the first time of the touch of the sun on her breasts and belly. The sensation was strange . . . and naughty . . . and she loved it.

"Not as often if the weather's bad"—his velvet voice gave added allure to the atmosphere—"but I try to make it when I can. We're pretty high up here and get our share of snow. A four-wheel-drive does wonders."

"Mmmmmm," she purred contentedly. "Nice." But her thoughts weren't on the snow in the mountains. Instead her senses were tuning in to the delicious warmth slowly spreading through her limbs as the sun warmed them. The ensuing silence was a companionable one, as had been the others they'd shared that weekend. But she felt Mark's gaze the instant it touched her and she opened a single eye to catch him in the act, propped up on an elbow and very near.

She was the one who was caught, however, ensnared in his circle of enchantment when he smiled at her. In that instant the gentle tickle of the breeze on her skin evolved into something far different and erotic, as did that slow-seeping golden warmth in her body. Her pulse stirred dangerously when his eyes made a leisurely perusal of her bare and slender length.

"Now, if I were the perfect hero," he drawled more thickly, "I'd whip out my trusty bottle of suntan lotion, squeeze a shameless amount in the palm of my hand and begin to very slowly and sensuously spread it over every sweet inch of you."

Deanna sucked in her breath. "Oh?"

"Uh-huh." He raised a hand and began to touch. "I'd dot it here"—her throat—"and smooth it here"—her arms—"and swirl it in a figure eight like this"—each breast in turn. She bit her lip to restrain a cry of delight. But he was far from done, though his own chest had begun a quickened rise and fall.

"Then I'd squirt more from the bottle and carefully coat your legs." His hand slid down the skin of her thigh and over the calf of one leg before bridging the gap between her ankles and retracing the parallel route.

"Mark!" she gasped, but he ignored her.

"If I were the perfect hero," he continued hoarsely, rolling her to her side to face him and acting out his words, "I'd cover your shoulders and your back, your bottom, then your legs, giving you a very skilled massage in the process.''

The arm she'd instinctively draped over his shoulder when he'd turned her tightened. His body was close enough to reveal the state of his arousal and it enlivened hers all the more. Her gaze fused with his. She couldn't have looked elsewhere had she tried.

"Then what?" she whispered, her heart pounding loudly when he let her lie back and rolled over. Her legs accommodated him eagerly.

"Then," he murmured huskily, unable to control the faint tremor that shimmered through his supporting arms, "I'd turn onto my back in a grand show of self-control . . . if I were the perfect hero. . . .''

She could barely keep from arching against him. "Well . . .?" Her breath came in shorter gasps as he moved above her.

His answer was a firm thrust that found her more than ready. "I'm not," he groaned, instants before he seized her lips and sought her fire.

She gave it unconditionally, drawing out each heady sensation to its fullest as she gloried in her ability to match Mark's passion spark for spark, flame for flame. She was without inhibition, freely crying out her pleasure as he'd taught her to do, demanding more and more from him. She was his equal on every plane and at times very much the guide, daring to show him her delights and demand his. Mark gave her his all, finally joining her in a blinding moment of rapture that each would treasure in memory through the long days to come.

# 9

**T**rue to his word, Mark returned her to Atlanta on Monday morning after awakening her with a melancholy kiss shortly after dawn. By nine o'clock she was on the fortieth floor of the Hunt International, soaking in a hot bath, wondering what she was going to do.

Mark had been remarkable. He hadn't pushed the issue of the future, perhaps knowing all too well that it was bound to close in on her without his help. At her request he had dropped her off at the front door of the hotel. He had made no fuss, been as quiet when they'd arrived as he'd been preoccupied during the drive. There were no kisses, no impassioned good-byes. Those had all been exchanged during the night. Now there was only the visual exchange that said so much.

"I'll give you your time," was all he said. "You call me when you're up to it."

Once more it was her choice. Hard as it was, that was one of the things she loved about Mark. He seemed to have the ultimate faith in her, and in turn, she believed herself worthy. She'd probably made more momentous decisions in the past month than she'd made in the past few years combined.

Now, submerged in scented water, it was time to make at least part of her decision. Could Mark fit into even her immediate future? More to the point, could she design that future to accommodate Mark? There was still the matter of the future in the far-reaching sense. Should Mark want marriage and children from her, that would be something completely different. But that was a bridge she hadn't come to yet and she refused to anticipate it. The days ahead were all that was on her mind for now.

Bob Warner had been perturbed, according to Irma's wry accounting, when he'd been unable to reach her on Saturday and then again on Sunday. There had been something about "very important clients" arriving on the spur of the moment and Deanna not being there to greet them.

"Too bad!" she fumed aloud, shifting position in the water. "He takes too much for granted." In all fairness, though, it was largely her own fault. For years she'd always been there, at the beck and call of the Hunt Foundation. Bob would have to understand that she now had other interests.

And she did. In essence, there was no decision to be made. She couldn't possibly let Mark Birmingham slip from her life, loving him as she did. Even if she couldn't give him everything he wanted, she'd discovered far too much about herself to ever go back to the insulated life she'd led. Being that much more of a person was worth every bit of the risk.

But being who she was, there were certain ways to do things. It certainly wouldn't do to invite an out-and-out confrontation with Bob any more than it would do to simply call Mark on the phone and announce that she'd decided that they could see each other publicly. Subtlety would be the preferable course.

Armed with this resolve, she returned to the daily pattern of Mrs. Lawrence Hunt. Only those who knew her well and saw her often noticed the heightened color in her cheeks. They also knew that all the complimenting, all the fishing in the world, would not weasel its cause from her. Deanna was indeed a very private person.

The week passed pleasantly enough for Deanna, with her glorious dreams of seeing Mark offsetting the loneliness of being without him. She was even pleased with her handling of Bob Warner, another feather in her cap of burgeoning self-confidence.

"I was put on quite a spot," he'd cautiously chastised her when they met in his office on Tuesday afternoon.

She'd kept calm, controlling her instinctive anger. She was far from a child, yet this man talked to her as though she were one, and a thoughtless one at that. "I'm sure you covered for me nicely."

"Oh, I covered for you, but Tom and Myra were disappointed. It was an embarrassing situation."

"Embarrassing?" Her eyebrows arched. "My having spent a weekend in the mountains?"

Bob's gaze narrowed. "Your having spent a weekend in the mountains with our architect."

"How did you know that?" She managed to temper her surprise. "Irma would never have—"

"Irma didn't have to tell me anything." He smiled smugly. "Hotel clerks see everything."

"Oh." Pondering this, she grew resentful of the tawdry way he'd painted the weekend. "But I don't see what difference it makes." Her eyes glittered defiantly. "Paperhanger, gardener, architect or financier, Mark is a friend of mine. I knew him even before you accepted his designs for the hospital."

Bob rose from the desk; it was his turn for surprise.

"You *knew* him? Then . . . that was nothing more than a well-acted scene in our conference room?"

"That's right." She held his gaze unflinchingly. It was about time he realized that he wasn't dealing with a simpleton.

"I see." He looked down at the straight line of buttons on his vest, then rocked back onto his heels. "Is there anything else I should know?"

"Uh-huh." She smiled more gently. "I think it would be a good idea for Mark to attend several of these dinner parties I've been conned into giving. If I'm to be a drawing card, he'd be an even stronger one." She stood, and didn't blink when she faced Bob. "The first party is a week from Thursday night. Would you please call him and extend the invitation on behalf of the foundation? Coming from you, it would be more official." She had her own reasons for the method. "If he's free, I'd very much like him to come. You can give me his answer whenever you get a chance." She shrugged. Then she turned on her heel, chin held high, and left, knowing that Bob Warner had just had his first glimpse of a woman who would no longer be content to be a decorative corporate insignia.

Despite her nonchalant show of confidence at the time, Deanna was on pins and needles as she waited to hear Mark's response. She half wished she'd made the call herself and eliminated the suspense, but it was part of her plan to have the overture come from Bob. She wanted it to be perfectly clear to everyone involved that Mark was there out of dedication to the project, rather than dedication to her.

But that was the stickler. Was he as dedicated to her as she wanted to believe? He hadn't called her and she didn't dare prod Bob on *his* success for fear he'd suspect her of having taken the easy way out. Had she? Had one small part of her been frightened—even after their loving weekend—that Mark would need the added incentive of a foundation affair to help him decide to come? Had Bob and the proposed hospital been her insurance?

It wasn't until she arrived at the office the following Tuesday, a full week later, that Bob let Mark's acceptance slip into the conversation. He could never have known the extent of her relief, engrossed as she was in a stack of grant proposals, but it was significant. The weekend before had seemed endless; her thoughts had been constantly on Mark. She had nearly given up hope, assuming that he was otherwise occupied, when Bob passed on the word that he'd be driving in from Savannah after an afternoon appointment and would be at her suite as early as he could make it.

Deanna was overjoyed. But instead of the next two days flying by, they were the longest she'd ever lived through. Everything had to be perfect for him—the table, the flowers, the wine and the menu. As in the past, the hotel kitchen catered the meal, the hotel florist provided the flowers and the hotel dining room provided one of its most skilled waiters for the evening. With Irma and Henry hard at work as well, there wasn't all that much for Deanna to do. That was perhaps the most frustrating thing of all.

Unwilling to feel helpless any longer, she made things for herself to do, small chores here and there to enhance the evening. Determined to make some sort of personal statement to Mark, she spent hours poring through Irma's stack of cookbooks, followed by hours in the kitchen turning a glossy photograph into reality. It was exhausting but fun, and she gained satisfaction from having played even a small role in the preparations.

Eight o'clock Thursday evening found Deanna looking elegant and exuberant in floor-length aqua chiffon and talking with her guests. Wine and hors d'oeuvres were in abundance, helping to fill time and stomachs until the last guest arrived. No one waited with breath as baited as Deanna's.

He came shortly before eight-thirty, with apologies all around for the tardiness that he blamed on a delayed start from Savannah. When he greeted Deanna, however, his smile was special, the gleam in his eye as meaningful as that in hers. Wildly in love as she was, Deanna made no bones about spending extra time with Mark, seating him by her side at dinner, turning from the others to him at every possible opportunity. Through it all though she was poised and dignified, adept in the art of hostessing. Only Bob Warner suspected that her interest in Mark was anything beyond solicitude toward the one man there who knew none of the others. That was, in fact, an irrelevant issue. As she'd known he would be, Mark was relaxed and totally self-assured among her guests. She couldn't help but admire him all the more for his polish.

Unfortunately, there were few opportunities for them to talk privately. At one point Mark was talking with another man, both of them seated on the sofa, when the other man was summoned across the room by his wife. Deanna dared go to the back of the sofa and bend over, close by Mark's ear.

"Did you taste the caviar pie?" she whispered.

"Delicious." He grinned, turning his head just the slightest bit toward her. "My compliments to the chef."

"I thank you," she rejoined with such pride that he couldn't have mistaken it in a million years.

"*You* made it?" he exclaimed. "That's great! But Irma must not be too thrilled with me."

"For turning me loose in her kitchen? You're right. She was, shall we say, dumbfounded. I think, though, that she was pretty pleased to have me stolen away to the country for the weekend." Even now Deanna recalled Irma's pleasure that the weekend had been a good one.

At her mention of that weekend, Mark grew more serious, his voice softer. "How are you?"

"Fine . . . You smell good." The faint scent of aftershave clung to his cheek.

"And you look beautiful," he returned, studying her keenly. "A little tired, I think."

"What do you expect?" She humored him. "I've spent the past two days planning and preparing one appetizer. You can bet that Bob was puzzled when I didn't show up at the office this afternoon." But Mark was right. She did feel tired, no doubt an emotional fatigue resulting from her wondering, worrying and waiting. "I'm glad you decided to come. I wasn't sure you would."

"Of course I'd come," he exclaimed. "Even on two days' notice!"

"Two days? That's ridiculous! I asked Bob to call you early last week!" Her voice held more than a touch of bewilderment.

Not so Mark's expression. He was clearly annoyed. "It looks like your Mr. Warner took his time about calling. Hmph! A subtle message if I ever got one! Somehow, I didn't peg him as the jealous type."

"Jealous? Of you?" She shot a glance at Bob, who was lingering in the dining room with his wife. "Bob's a married man!"

"That's not what I mean, Deanna. When it comes to you and the Hunt Foundation, he seems to be very possessive."

"You're right about that." She grimaced. "When he wanted me for something the other weekend and discovered that I wasn't here, he was pretty upset."

Mark grew concerned. "Oh, honey, I'm sorry. Did he give you a hard time?"

Deanna grinned mischievously. "You would've been proud of me. I stood up to him quite well. He was almost as amazed as I was! But come on." Straightening, she held out her hand. "I think we'd better mingle."

Mingle they did, primarily discussing the hospital project and its needs until nearly midnight, when the last of the talk died away and the final couple, Bob and his wife, left. Mark stayed behind with Deanna, partly out of defiance, partly out of concern.

"You look pale," he announced as soon as the front door was firmly shut. "You're sure you feel all right?"

"Just tired." She smiled wanly as she tucked her arm through his and led him back toward the living room. "I'll sleep in tomorrow." She paused, then spoke more hesitantly. "Will you . . . will you stay?"

"Here? Tonight?" he asked softly, finally beginning to understand how far she'd come. "God, Deanna, what a night to ask!"

"You won't?"

"I *can't.* I have a very early appointment that I wasn't able to change on such short notice."

"In Atlanta?"

"In Savannah." Now Deanna finally began to understand how far *he'd* come. But he went on. "Besides, I don't think you'd make it past the first couple of kisses. What you need far more than me is sleep."

Despite her disappointment, she had to agree with him. She'd been tired all week and needed the rest now that this first party was over and an unqualified success. Two of the men present had promised to send Bob substantial checks in the morning. As for Deanna, she was planning to spend her morning sleeping and had already told LeeAnn not to look for her at the club.

"Then I won't see you until next week?" she asked, feeling suddenly lonesome again.

"Next week?" Mark eyed her blankly.

"Oh, no! Didn't Bob tell you about *that?*" When he

shook his head she gritted her teeth. "He really must have a problem. The second party's a week from tonight. I had hoped you'd come to that one too." Her gaze held the invitation that was supposed to have been issued long since.

Mark fell victim to the plea and took her in his arms, seeming to be temporarily satisfied to overlook Bob's omission. "I think that you need a dinner partner"—he grinned—"and I'm the only one around."

"If it was a simple dinner partner I needed"—she grinned back, undaunted—"I'd choose from among the many very wealthy divorcés in the area. Then, while he was here, I'd drain him of his fortune in true black-widow fashion."

He feigned a shudder to match her exaggerated drawl. "Not you at all, Deanna. I guess I'll just *have* to come preserve your character."

She slid her arms around his neck and rested her head on his shoulder. "What you do to me does nothing to preserve my character! Mmmmmm, I could stay like this all night."

"And I'd never make it to my appointment," he crooned softly. "Deanna?"

"Mmmmmm?" Her eyes were closed and she felt totally peaceful.

"Can I see you this weekend?"

When her head bobbed back up her eyes were filled with excitement. "I'd love that," she whispered, knowing that his question held a meaning far deeper than the actual words and pleased that she could finally accept the challenge.

Mark arrived shortly after noon on Saturday and stayed through Sunday evening. During that time he and Deanna spent every minute together. They walked through the city hand in hand, with Deanna uncaring of who should see. They ate at the suite and they ate out. They visited the modern-art museum, then took a carriage ride through downtown Atlanta. It was something that Deanna, for all her years in Atlanta, had never done, something very much for tourists, something undeniably romantic.

Best of all was the fact that they had hour after hour alone. Irma had made up the guest room for Mark, unaware—or perhaps simply discreet and accepting—that Deanna would be spending Saturday night in that large bed with him. It was there that they talked quietly of past and present, avoiding the future as something neither was yet ready to handle. They made love and slept, then repeated the pattern until Deanna gave way to exhaustion. It was, ironically, this that later caused the only minor friction between them.

"You're still tired?" He frowned at her, noting her lagging pace when they returned to the suite after an early dinner Sunday evening.

Deanna flopped down onto the sofa. "You've worn me out."

"We slept all morning." he argued,

"Maybe it's the exercise," she shot back suggestively. Not only had they walked for miles, but their night had indeed been punctuated by intermittent activity.

But Mark was serious. "I think you should see a doctor. You're still pale and I don't like it."

"I'm fine," she insisted.

"Deanna?" He had come to sit by her side.

"Uh-oh. I'm beginning to recognize that tone of voice."

Ignoring her flippancy, he reached out to tuck a stray strand of hair behind her ear. She had worn it down just for him. "Deanna, I have to ask you something."

She took his hand and held it between hers, put her head back and shut her eyes. This lethargy had begun to bother her too, but she refused to worry Mark with it. "Mmmmm?"

"I was wondering . . . I mean, I know I should have asked you before . . ."

Puzzled by his hesitancy and the trouble he seemed to be having, she raised her head and looked at him. "What is it?"

With a sigh he spoke. "You went through nine years of marriage without a child, so I more or less assumed you used some form of protection. It's been over a month since we were first together. You're suddenly more tired than usual. Do you think you could be pregnant?"

She hadn't expected this; she'd pushed all thought of her inability to conceive from her mind. Mark's abrupt broaching of the subject left her momentarily speechless. And try as she might, she couldn't decipher his expression.

"Pregnant?" she squeaked, then cleared her throat, returning her voice to a more normal pitch. There was no point in prevarication. "No. I'm not pregnant," she declared with such finality that he didn't raise the possibility again. He did, however, harp on her health to the extent that by the time he was ready to leave she was on edge.

"Promise me you'll see a doctor?" he asked as he stood by the door, his overnight bag in hand.

She shook her head. "There's no need."

"Just a checkup?"

"Mark"—she sighed—"I had a checkup last spring. I'm fine."

"For *my* sake?"

"No! You're making a mountain out of a molehill. Now, if you'd leave already, I could get some sleep!" The last thing she wanted was for him to leave, but a drawn-out farewell promised to devastate her.

"Promise you *will* rest?"

"Yes, Mark," she drawled, rolling her eyes toward the ceiling.

"And I'll see you Thursday?"

"Yes." This more gently.

"Be good," he murmured and was gone.

With the exception of a nervous stomach she felt fine by Thursday, having convinced herself that several days' pampering was all she needed. It puzzled her that she was apprehensive about this week's party, more so than the last. Her only possible excuse lay in her relative unfamiliarity with this group of potential donors. But Bob and his wife would be there again, and, of course, Mark. Her stomach fluttered at that thought in a way that was far from nervous. Though he had to leave again for a prescheduled meeting in Savannah on Friday morning, he'd rearranged his plans for Thursday afternoon so that he was able to drive in earlier. That gave them time to talk before the guests arrived, to fill each other in on the week's events.

"You look better today," he was quick to comment.

Deanna chuckled. "I should hope so. I slept through most of Monday and even some of Tuesday. I'm sure your week had to be more interesting."

Relieved by her apparent revival, he dropped the issue. Deanna, however, was unable to do so as easily, because as the late afternoon wore on into early evening she felt queasy. And her dilemma was a twofold one—coping with that queasiness and simultaneously hiding it from Mark.

She was at least temporarily successful on both counts. Slowly sipping her wine, she prayed that it would either settle her stomach or numb her to her uneasiness. She nibbled on an hors d'oeuvre or two, but didn't dare eat more. And she was pleasantly surprised and infinitely grateful when it turned out that Mark knew several of the guests she didn't. He easily took that added weight from her shoulders.

She managed to appear composed and charming through the cold strawberry soup that was served first, even survived the shrimp mornay without much more than a twinge. She purposely made light of Mark's growing concern.

"You're not eating," he murmured beneath his breath.

"You sound like my father."

"I'm serious, Deanna. Are you okay?"

"I think my insides are a little too stirred up to eat." She pacified him with a quick smile.

A few minutes later he reached under the tablecloth for her hand. "God, you feel clammy. Are you sure you wouldn't like to lie down for a while?"

"I can't just run out of here, Mark. Besides, it's nothing. I'll be fine once I get some coffee into me."

She didn't make it that far. Just before dessert was served, at a point where, as hostess, her absence could be easily explained, she quietly excused herself, walked smoothly from the room, breaking into a run only when she was well out of sight.

She reached the bathroom in time to be violently ill. When Mark suddenly materialized beside her she felt neither embarrassment nor humiliation, only relief and a wealth of gratitude. He seemed to know exactly what to do and say . . . as well as what not to say. It was no time for "I-told-you-so's."

When she'd lost all there was to lose he helped her freshen up. "Why don't you rest here for a few minutes?" he suggested softly. "I'll cover for you."

She wouldn't hear of it. "No. I really feel much better now. As long as I don't eat, I think I'll be fine."

Mark didn't argue. Had she studied him closely she would have seen the tension in his jaw and known that the argument would come later. But her main concern at the moment was forgetting that she'd been sick, and she *did* feel greatly improved. Even her legs didn't wobble much when she stood to return to the dining room.

At the bedroom door she turned back. "Thanks, Mark." She smiled softly up at him. "I don't know what I would have done without you just now." Self-sufficiency was one thing, and had its own set of rewards, she realized. But being able to depend on another human being, having that other human being there when you needed him—that was just as beautiful. Somehow, in her move to break from the past, she'd overlooked that.

"You'd have lived," he murmured with a look of resignation as he cocked his head toward the door. "Lead on."

The rest of the evening was as uneventful as Deanna had wanted it to be. Though still weak, she felt much better. The fact that Bob Warner kept an eagle eye on her she attributed to the jealousy Mark had suggested. Mark himself stayed close beside her all evening, watching her keenly, playing the solicitous dinner partner to perfection. He was for all intents and purposes the ideal host, in spite of the thin line of tension that made him graver than usual.

This gravity was never heavier than when the door closed at last and they were alone. Knowing what was coming, Deanna bowed her head, walked to the nearest chair and sank down, letting her weariness cushion her against the imminent attack. It was surprisingly brief.

"All right, Deanna. Will you see a doctor tomorrow or do I have to drag you?"

"It's just some kind of bug, Mark. Nothing to get upset about."

"Well I *am* upset! Now what will it be . . . willing or unwilling?"

His mind was set. Lifting her head to look at him, Deanna couldn't miss the rock hardness of his brown-eyed gaze. Nor could she miss the thick auburn hair brushed to docility, the jaw clean-shaven and strong, the lips of thin and manly set. She loved him so much. He *had* to have her best interests at heart.

"I'll go." She capitulated in a low whisper.

"What was that?" He arched one brow, having obviously heard the first time but demanding greater conviction.

She gave it helplessly. "I'll go!"

# 10

~~~~~~~~~~~

**D**eanna sat stunned in the backseat of the car, still unable to believe what the doctor had just told her.

"Where to, Mrs. Hunt?" Henry's voice broke through her daze.

Her eyes met his in the rearview mirror. "Uh, home, I guess." Then she added on impulse, "But will you take the long way, Henry? It's a beautiful day."

Indeed it was, with the sun shining brightly along the light stone-and-glass face of the city. She rolled down her window and let the breeze blow the soft tendrils around her face to complement her gentle smile.

Pregnant! She was actually pregnant! How many years she'd waited, wanted to hear those words! Mark had been right after all. He'd known the signs better than she had. But no—that wasn't it. She'd just refused to read them for fear they'd prove to be a false alarm.

As the car wound smoothly through the curving tree-lined streets skirting the central city, she tried to sort out her thoughts. Pregnant. She was overwhelmed by its unexpectedness, terrified by its magnitude. Somehow, though, nothing could blunt the abundant joy she felt. To be carrying a child, a love child, Mark's child—it gave the word *luxury* another meaning.

Henry could only drive around for so long. When he pulled up at the hotel, though, Deanna still wasn't ready to go inside. In spite of the fatigue, which the doctor had said would pass, and the intermittent nausea, for which he'd given her a prescription, she felt positively glowing and wonderfully alive. She had her own very precious secret growing inside and she would have liked nothing more than to scream it to the world.

*That,* unfortunately, she couldn't do. In fact, there was apt to be all hell to pay in terms of her image as the saintly Hunt widow. Her image . . . right now she couldn't have cared less! This was *her* life, *her* child. Somehow she'd find the answers for everything.

"Tell Irma I'll be in for lunch a little later," she told Henry when he helped her from the car. "I'm taking a walk."

Wasn't this how so much of her new outlook had begun—that walk she'd taken on that rainy afternoon? Now it was a radiant noontime. There were people all about, walking more leisurely in appreciation of the glorious weather.

She made an aimless circle through the downtown streets, ambling slowly, smiling all the way, thinking no further than the delight of the moment. Pregnant! She still couldn't believe it! What would Mark say?

Up to this moment she'd taken her pregnancy as a kind of personal victory, made doubly sweet because of the years she'd thought herself barren, the weeks she'd thought herself unworthy of Mark and his future. Mark had *truly* brought her to her full potential, she mused as she turned and headed toward home. What was to be done now? What would *he* want to do?

She was unprepared for the air of confrontation that hung heavy in the suite when she arrived. No sooner had she let herself in, closed the door behind her and turned, than she gasped, eyes widening instantly to take in both men.

"Mark . . . Bob . . . what are you two doing here?"

One was on his feet as quickly as the next, advancing on her with concern—no, anger. In a moment of *déjà vu* Deanna recalled a similar scene when she'd returned to find Mark in a fury. He wasn't much calmer now.

"Well?" He planted himself before her, legs wide in determination, hands on his hips.

"What are *you* doing here?" she asked. "I thought you were back in Savannah?"

"Fool that I was, I was worried. I decided to stay over here at the hotel last night and called Savannah first thing this morning to cancel my meeting. Then I took the elevator up here to make sure you'd gone to the doctor. I was waiting very patiently until your sidekick here showed up." He cocked his head toward Bob, but his eyes never left Deanna. "I *asked* you if it was a possibility and you told me it wasn't!"

Deanna was still trying to grasp the fact of this un-planned tête-à-tête and Mark's uncanny knowledge when Bob coralled her attention. His attitude was blatantly condemnatory.

"How could you have done this, Deanna? You're the showpiece of the foundation!"

Gripped by a sudden and overwhelming anger, Deanna was speechless. To have her bubble of excite-ment burst in such a cold and insensitive way was unfair! But before she could vent her indignation Mark beat her to the punch. He turned to face Bob.

"*Showpiece?* The woman is flesh and blood, not a statue on a pedestal!"

"Whatever," Bob retaliated in a low, rumbling voice. "She's very important to the image of the foundation. How does it look now that she's publicly taken up with someone and is pregnant with his child to boot!"

Deanna's head flew back to Mark, her stomach churning as she heard his low-seethed "She'll be married to me before anyone knows anything! It's my child and I take full responsibility for it. I may not be the foundation, but I believe I have *some* rights here!"

"*Wait just a minute!*" Deanna screamed, holding her shaking hands palms out, stepping back unsteadily. She looked from man to man, unbelieving of what was happening. She paused to try to catch her breath, but found that to be impossible, so she went on anyway. "I'd like to know what you both think you're doing! I'm not some total imcompetent whose future needs to be mapped out for her. At least . . . not anymore!"

"That was what *I* thought," Bob broke in, "until this happened. Where was your common sense? It's simple enough for a woman to prevent this kind of thing nowadays!"

She saw red. "What an ignorantly chauvinistic thing to say! And you really don't know the facts, Bob."

"Okay, Deanna," he granted, "I have to admit that you may be new at this. What with Larry's condition, you didn't have to worry about becoming pregnant."

Her breath caught in a soft hiss as time was suspended for an instant. "What did you say?" she whispered tremulously. Mark took in her pallor before following her gaze to Bob's face.

"I'm sorry." Bob scowled. "I'm sure it's hard to think back on that. It nearly broke Larry's heart to discover he was sterile."

"My God!" she mouthed the words, finally understanding how truly mistaken she'd been about her own capabilities. "Sterile? I . . . I never knew." She was far too shocked to derive any satisfaction from Bob's sudden remorse.

"He never told you?" he asked more quietly.

She shook her head, her eyes wide, her vision blurring. "Did he . . . did he know all along?"

"No. He had tests only after you'd been married for several years. I guess he didn't have the courage to tell you."

Clutching her middle, she looked down to the floor. "All these years I thought *I* was the one who couldn't have children. . . ." She pressed a fist to her mouth, but wrenched it out to hold Mark off when he started to put his arm around her. Sensing her need to work something out, he stepped back.

Deanna wasn't sure whether to break down or explode. It seemed a toss-up, given the maelstrom of emotions that twisted her insides. How could Larry have kept the truth from her? But he was gone now and couldn't answer the question. Frustrated, she turned on Bob.

"You seem to be privy to all sorts of information that by rights you shouldn't know. If it wouldn't be too rude of me to ask, how did *you* come to be here this morning?"

"When I called here Irma told me you'd gone to the doctor."

"Surely she didn't name the doctor . . . ?"

"No." He shifted his stance uncomfortably. "I checked with Dr. Renswicke."

"Our family doctor . . . clever. And when he said I didn't have an appointment with *him* . . . ?"

"He knew the name of your gynecologist. Wolson's office confirmed that you'd been there. No, they wouldn't pass on any news . . . but it was easy enough to guess, given the circumstances." He shot a wary glance toward Mark, then looked back to Deanna. "At least you knew which doctor to see."

"I'm not that stupid, Bob," she snapped, "even if I *have* been misled all these years!" She lowered her head and took a deep breath. "That's quite a list. Irma. Doctors Renswicke and Wolson. The *hotel clerks.*" When she trembled this time it was in pure anger. It took every ounce of her strength to keep her fury in check. Her gaze, though, held a venom Bob couldn't possibly have escaped. "From what I can see, Bob, you've used my own people against me. Perhaps you forget that the Hunt Foundation is mine, that Larry left it to me. You may be its executive director but you don't, you *can't,* direct my life. After all the years in which I've given the foundation my loyalty you have no right to even suggest that I've shirked my responsibility." She'd never lashed out so strongly at anyone and she found the power heady. "I've been perfectly satisfied with the job you've done as executive director, but so help me, if you ever, *ever* again try to interfere with my personal life, I'll have you looking for a position before you can think to resign."

She was nearly breathless, but barely paused when she caught Mark's satisfied grin. "And as for *you.*" She turned to him and his grin vanished. "I'll have you know that this is *my* baby in *my* body." Her voice rose despite her efforts to contain it. Where Mark was concerned her heart was deeply involved. "I have the means to raise it in comfort all by myself and that may well be what I do!" Her eyes filled with tears, but she didn't care. "All I know is that I don't regret a thing!"

"Deanna—" Mark began, only to be interrupted.

"You've taught me that I'm a very special person, a woman, an individual who can think and function."

"Deanna—"

"*I'm not done,* Mark!" she sobbed angrily, her cheeks

wet. "And you can *both* hear this. I won't have anyone telling me what to do again. I have a mind. From now on, I'm making my own decisions." She jabbed a finger at Bob. "You won't *tell* me that I should tailor my love life to the needs of the foundation any more than *you*"—the finger turned toward Mark—"will *tell* me I'm going to marry you. *I* make the decisions for *me* and I think I've got enough common sense to make the right ones. She straightened and inhaled raggedly. "Now, if you gentlemen will excuse me, I feel sick!"

"Deanna . . . !" Mark tried again but she was already half way down the hall, headed for her bedroom. Her exit had been unbelievably regal and he didn't know whether to be proud or frustrated.

As for Deanna, she collapsed on the bed in a state of numbed exhaustion. The events of the morning blended together into a hazy cloud hovering over her head. Lying on her side with her knees tucked up, she buried her face against the pillow and waited for something, anything, to penetrate the mist.

"I love you, Deanna." She heard his words, felt the bed give beneath his weight, but still wasn't sure that she hadn't dreamed it. "I do love you. Didn't I tell you that once?"

"In your sleep," she whispered without opening her eyes.

"I wasn't sleeping. I knew exactly what I was saying. But I thought I'd be rushing you . . . and then there's this life you have where you don't need a thing . . ."

She opened her eyes then and raised them to his. In that moment she saw the same vulnerability she'd seen so often and all her anger vanished. "I need *you*," she murmured and her arms went around him as he lifted her. "And I like to think that you need me just as much as our baby will, come next spring. For the first time in my life I feel . . . complete. I love you." She knew it for a fact despite the tears that blurred her vision. The beauty of the moment's confession was no dream.

"Ahhhhh, Deanna." He shuddered and held her closer. "Are you sure? You're not just wanting to feel that way because of the baby?"

Her hand joined his against her abdomen. "I've loved you for days, Mark—long before I found out about the baby."

"Why didn't you tell me? I've waited and waited . . . I'd told you and I needed some encouragement. . . ."

Deanna was touched by the depth of his fear, enough to confess her own. "I was frightened that you'd demand a commitment I didn't feel at the time I could live up to."

"But surely you must have guessed you were pregnant. . . ."

"No!" She pulled back to face him, recalling the shock she'd suffered earlier. "I knew there was a problem when I was late . . . and then so sick. But I assumed there was another cause. You heard what I told Bob." Her voice trembled. "I honestly thought I was incapable of having children. And it was one of the reasons I fought against a future with you. It was bad enough that I was a novice of a cook and a housekeeper, but you wanted, you deserved, a family . . . and I thought I couldn't give you one."

Mark smiled gently. "But you know better now."

"I do," she whispered, mirroring his smile before snuggling against him once more. "Mmmmmm, I love you so much. . . ."

"You'd better," he rasped, his lips warm against her forehead. "Because I'm going to *ask* you to marry me and if you accept my proposal it will mean changing this life of yours a little."

Deanna tipped her head back again. "You don't have to marry me because of the baby, Mark. If that's the reason, it would never work."

"I love you. *That's* the reason I want to marry you. I've wanted to ask you for days now, but I thought you weren't ready. The baby might have been my excuse for pressuring you if all else failed, but I wanted it to be your decision, freely made." He grinned. "And after that outburst in the other room, I do think you'd have the baby all by yourself if you so decided."

"I would. See what a taste of real life has done to me?"

"I love it," he quipped, then kissed her soundly. "But you will marry me, won't you?"

That old vulnerability was back and it did melting things to her. "Yes."

"For the baby's sake?"

"For *my* sake. I have this absurd need to protect you from the world."

"When?"

"When will I protect you?" she teased with an aura of innocence.

"When will you *marry* me?" he growled, administering a playfully gruff squeeze.

Smiling, Deanna rested her head against his chest. "I'll leave that decision up to you."

"Hey . . . I thought you wanted to be the decision maker."

"Not *the* decision maker. *A* decision maker. Right now I'm tired enough to welcome any help I can get."

"Deanna?" His breath fanned her hair.

"Mmmmmm?"

"Are you sure you're ready for this? For a while there you were so worried about the foundation and your role in it."

"That was before, thanks to you, I discovered *me*. I think I used the foundation as an excuse, something to hide behind. I'd begun to realize something was missing in my life—"

"That's not what you told *me*!"

"You bet your sexy briefs it wasn't! You frightened me—or rather, it was the strength of my feelings for you that frightened me. And those terrible feelings of inadequacy. I was so sure I didn't have the wherewithal to make you happy."

His arms tightened convulsively around her. "Oh, Deanna, I love you," he moaned with such depth of feeling that she had to believe him. "You're all I've ever wanted in a woman."

"And you really canceled your appointments today on *my* account?"

"Sure did. But you sound surprised. Isn't that what you did for me when I abducted you for a weekend in the mountains?"

"Hmmmmm." She chuckled. "Different kinds of appointments . . . but I suppose you've got a point." She burrowed closer against the firmness of his chest. "That was a wonderful weekend."

"Want to go back?"

She sat up. "Say when."

"When." He grinned rakishly.

"Really?"

"Sure. I'd say you could use a good weekend's rest what with all this unplanned excitement." He darted a glance at his watch. "We could leave right after lunch, if you can be ready by then."

"I'm ready now."

"I thought you felt sick."

"Not anymore."

"Speedy recovery?"

"The best medicine in the world."

"I love you," he whispered, his eyes filled with adoration.

"That's it!" She laughed, and opened her heart for another dose.

# YOU'LL BE SWEPT AWAY
# WITH SILHOUETTE DESIRE

### $1.75 each

1 ☐ CORPORATE AFFAIR
James

2 ☐ LOVE'S SILVER WEB
Monet

3 ☐ WISE FOLLY
Clay

4 ☐ KISS AND TELL
Carey

5 ☐ WHEN LAST WE LOVED
Baker

6 ☐ A FRENCHMAN'S KISS
Mallory

7 ☐ NOT EVEN FOR LOVE
St. Claire

8 ☐ MAKE NO PROMISES
Dee

9 ☐ MOMENT IN TIME
Simms

10 ☐ WHENEVER I LOVE YOU
Smith

### $1.95 each

11 ☐ VELVET TOUCH
James

12 ☐ THE COWBOY AND THE
LADY    Palmer

13 ☐ COME BACK, MY LOVE
Wallace

14 ☐ BLANKET OF STARS
Valley

15 ☐ SWEET BONDAGE
Vernon

16 ☐ DREAM COME TRUE
Major

17 ☐ OF PASSION BORN
Simms

18 ☐ SECOND HARVEST
Ross

19 ☐ LOVER IN PURSUIT
James

20 ☐ KING OF DIAMONDS
Allison

21 ☐ LOVE INTHE CHINA SEA
Baker

22 ☐ BITTERSWEET IN BERN
Durant

23 ☐ CONSTANT STRANGER
Sunshine

24 ☐ SHARED MOMENTS
Baxter

25 ☐ RENAISSANCE MAN
James

26 ☐ SEPTEMBER MORNING
Palmer

27 ☐ ON WINGS OF NIGHT
Conrad

28 ☐ PASSIONATE JOURNEY
Lovan

29 ☐ ENCHANTED DESERT
Michelle

30 ☐ PAST FORGETTING
Lind

31 ☐ RECKLESS PASSION
James

32 ☐ YESTERDAY'S DREAMS
Clay

38 ☐ SWEET SERENITY
Douglass

39 ☐ SHADOW OF BETRAYAL
Monet

40 ☐ GENTLE CONQUEST
Mallory

41 ☐ SEDUCTION BY DESIGN
St. Claire

42 ☐ ASK ME NO SECRETS
Stewart

43 ☐ A WILD, SWEET MAGIC
Simms

44 ☐ HEART OVER MIND West

45 ☐ EXPERIMENT IN LOVE Clay

46 ☐ HER GOLDEN EYES Chance

47 ☐ SILVER PROMISES Michelle

48 ☐ DREAM OF THE WEST
Powers

49 ☐ AFFAIR OF HONOR James

## Silhouette Desire

# Enjoy your own special time with Silhouette Romances.

## Send for 6 books today— one is yours <u>free</u>!

Silhouette Romances take you into a special world of thrilling drama, tender passion, and romantic love. These are enthralling stories from your favorite romance authors—tales of fascinating men and women, set in exotic locations all over the world.

**Convenient free home delivery.** We'll send you six exciting Silhouette Romances to look over for 15 days. If you enjoy them as much as we think you will, pay the invoice enclosed with your trial shipment. **One book is yours free to keep.** Silhouette Romances are delivered right to your door with never a charge for postage or handling. There's no minimum number of books to buy, and you may cancel at any time.

*Silhouette Romances*

Silhouette Book Club® Dept. SRSD 7R
120 Brighton Road, Clifton, NJ 07012

Please send me 6 Silhouette Romances absolutely free, to look over for 15 days. If not delighted, I will return only 5 and owe nothing. **One book is mine free.**

NAME_____

ADDRESS_____

CITY_____

STATE_____ ZIP_____

SIGNATURE_____
(If under 18, parent or guardian must sign.)

This offer expires March 31, 1984

Silhouette Book Club® is a registered trademark of Simon & Schuster

# *READERS' COMMENTS ON SILHOUETTE DESIRES*